I'll Tell You a Love Story

© 2020 Couri Johnson

The stories in this collection were previously published in the following publications: "Tale Telling" in *Syntax and Salt*; "My Darling, Where Have You Gone?" in *Dark Lane Anthology 7*; "Thursday" in *Broken Pencil Magazine*; "Wolf's Wake" in *Print Oriented Bastards*; "Dancing Girls" in *Weird City*; "Curlew" in *Psycho Pomp*; "I'll Tell You a Love Story" in *Bone Parade*; "The Woman the Spiders Loved" in *Penultimate Peanut*; "Anatomist" in *Orba/Artifact*; "This is Where You Leave Me" in *littledeathlit;* "The Center of Everything" in *Cagibi*.

Published by Bridge Eight Press
Jacksonville, Florida

All rights reserved.

www.bridgeeight.com

ISBN 978-1-7323667-5-6
EISBN 978-1-7323667-6-3
LCCN 2019957034

Printed in the USA
Distributed by Small Press Distribution
Cover & book design by Jared Rypkema

For Matthew Lattanzi and my mother, Janet Chapin Johnson

Stories

- **3** Tale Telling
- **15** My Darling, Where Have You Gone?
- **33** Thursday
- **37** Ten Things I'm Irrationally Afraid Of (Listed in No Particular Order)
- **41** Wolf's Wake
- **51** Dancing Girls
- **71** Curlew
- **83** I'll Tell You a Love Story
- **89** Outbound
- **117** The Woman the Spiders Loved
- **119** Miloslav
- **139** Anatomist
- **157** The Way of the Dinosaurs
- **161** This is Where You Leave Me
- **175** The Center of Everything

I'll Tell You a Love Story

Tale Telling

DOWNTOWN THERE'S A BUILDING WITH PLASTIC DOGS DOTTING ITS roof. It's a dump, really. Squat, ugly, painted rust red and old-coffee-stain yellow in a way that suggests one of the colors was slapped on 'cause they ran out of the first. Outside it says it's a post office museum and a thrift store. The roof is made of tin shingles that look like halved cans of beans, and the dogs all look the same, sitting stiff and obedient, with their mouths open in anticipation, and their eyes cast upward at an invisible master they adore.

There were maybe a dozen of the dogs the weekend I first met you. The building was just outside of the nice part of town. I passed by it on my way to where we'd be meeting, and there was something in my heart that wasn't exactly anxiety or excitement. The closest I can come to explaining it is by saying I felt a little like a teenager. But that's not true either. It had been a long time since I had felt anything like being young.

See, I think aging works like this: time is like these drops of water pouring steadily into you. Each moment adds up and adds up until inside you're flooded, right? And everything just starts feeling damp and sluggish and heavy. The worse the moment, the heavier the downpour.

I was already at a point that was full to burst when we met. And I think I envied those dogs. I could tell from the way the light shone through them that there was nothing inside weighing them down.

There's a story I read when I was younger about this girl who'd loved this man. They were wed, but something went wrong. She did something she ought not have, and so he had to leave. He didn't even want to exactly, but that's the way it had to be. As further penance she had to wear iron shoes that cut her with every step she took. And she took a lot. After he left, she walked the world looking for him. She climbed ice cliffs, walked deserts, and nearly drowned wading through rivers.

There are lots of stories out there like that. So many that folklorists gave them their own classification: The Search for the Lost Husband. One of its earliest incarnations is this myth about the Goddess Freyja. She slept with a bunch of dwarves for this golden necklace. When she returned home, her husband was gone. She got in her chariot and rode for ages, searching for him, but she never did see him again.

Sometimes, that happens.

But this girl found her husband. He took the shoes off her, and he took her back. But by then they were both old, and her feet were nothing more than ribbons of torn muscle and bone peeking through. The skin was all gone. And I guess that's always what I thought love was. Something you had to search and suffer for that would flay you to the bone.

We met at a hotel known for the creeping ivy that choked its walls. The place looked like the backdrop of a Victorian period piece, but it was only a five-minute walk down the street from that shop with the dogs. This was a place only people with money could afford to stay, and even the small café on the first floor operated outside of my means. But it was a nice place to meet. In the courtyard sat a fountain in the middle of the cobblestone pathway, and rose bushes lined the walls. It was the end of winter though, so they weren't much more than bundles of twigs twisting out of the ground. But it seemed like the right kind of place to meet someone, and I was trying to arrange things to be just right. Like that could make things turn out good. Or at the very least, keep them from going too bad.

The first time I saw you, you were standing in the courtyard, looking into the fountain with a coin perched on your thumb and index finger. When you saw me come toward you, you put the coin back in your pocket and came forward to shake my hand instead. I thought that maybe this could work.

That night we stayed up drinking. We talked. I put my mouth to yours, and each time your lips parted it felt a little like the water inside me was emptying out. Wherever you touched, it felt like my skin was peeling away until I was nothing more than bone. And I thought that maybe that meant something.

But maybe those aren't things to be thinking or doing or feeling during the first night of knowing someone.

On my walk home, the wind picked up, and I watched the dogs waver on the roof, as if at any moment they might take off like kites.

Other stories have girls set up opposite lovers who start out detestable. Girls carried away from their homes on the backs of bears, dogs, and pigs, and alienated until their love heals whatever ailment is making the man inside a monster. The most famous of these, of course, is "Beauty and the Beast," which is also the name folklorists gave to these kinds of tales.

I spent a lot of time with stories like that when I was growing up. Now that I'm older, people talk about Stockholm syndrome. They talk about gas lighting, and conditioning. It's not romance, they say now. It's abuse.

And I guess that's true.

There was this one story about a girl who'd been taken away from her family by a little short-toothed hound. She would beg him all the time to take her home, and each time he would agree, carry her within a few feet and let her off his back. When she approached the house he would ask her what he called himself, and she would say, "Dearest." Then he would ask what she called him, and she would tell him "mangy cur," or "trash fur," or "the worst thing that's ever fucking happened to me in my life." And she would run. She would get so close that her fingertips would brush the doorknob, and then the dog would snatch her by the back of her shirt and drag her all the way back to his home. It only stopped when she finally accepted him, and called him the name he wanted. Then he turned into a man, and they lived happily ever after, despite all of that still being a shitty thing to do to someone.

I guess you do what you have to when you're too broken to fix yourself.

And maybe there's a part of me that never really learned love wasn't about being brutal and ugly. About being isolating. About being a little terrifying.

And so maybe that's why I wasn't surprised when it happened

to us.

We developed a routine of it. Meet, go home together, drink as it grew dark, until it grew light and pour ourselves into each other. At first it seemed natural enough. Spring was slow in coming, and when it started to come at all, it came in angry. Winds, rains, the constant threat of a hurricane looming off coast. It was best just to take cover and huddle up under a blanket with a bottle of liquor to split between the two of us. It was a month and a half in that I started to worry maybe this wasn't enough for you. It was about a month and a half in that I started to feel things weren't pouring out, but pouring back in.

This started to sit wrong with me on our walk toward your place, and I stopped to look up at those dogs again. As a precaution against the weather, the shopkeeper had run a series of bungee cords from one end of the roof to the other and wrapped them around the bodies and necks of the dogs. On the side of the building, the ladder was still leaning against the roof. The wind kept kicking the dogs up to strain against the cords.

"Do you want to go in?" you asked.

I was so worried saying no would lead to you leaving that I went along with it.

Inside was lit by a single lamp in the corner behind the counter, at which a short, rotundish woman sat flipping through a magazine. All the merchandise was piled on tables set just far enough apart to make aisles. We walked through them, picking up this old thing and that. There were mostly chipped, scuffed, or cracked and all obviously trash.

"Where's the post office museum?" I asked.

The woman at the counter looked up at me with a scowl on her face, and struggled to her feet. She came around the counter and moved a curtain away from what I'd assumed was a window. Behind it was a narrow door made of plywood with a slot cut in the wood about halfway up, and a hole where the doorknob should be.

She turned and looked us up and down. "Five bucks a head," she told us. We looked at each other. You shrugged and reached for your wallet. When she was paid, she hooked her finger through the hole and dragged the plywood door forward in a way that made it grind against the floor. From out behind it poured envelopes and folded pieces of paper. The woman kicked them back in, and then stepped aside so we could slink through. She came in, and pulled a cord attached to a bare light bulb hanging above our head.

The whole room was about the size of two public restroom stalls. Along the walls there were shelves divided into cubby holes, some filled with old bronze stamps and silver scales, most of them warped and blackened. Others were filled with letters. Some of the letters were burnt and browned. Some were yellowed by age. Others were white as movie snow. The cubbies were stuffed full, and letters spilled out all over the floor. They crumpled under our feet like leaves as we stepped into the enclosed space and looked around.

On the wall was a plaque that you read aloud at a half-whisper:

"Once a city post office stood here, until a fire burned it down in 1944, claiming the lives of three postmen and destroying a majority of the letters. Most of the letters were missives from the army notifying the families of recently deceased soldiers. Ignorant of their own loss, the families went on writing letter after letter to the dead, until the end of the war came, and the soldiers never returned. But neither had their letters.

"After, people began to bring letters to the wrecked post office for those who had passed on. The belief was that the deceased postmen would continue to deliver them, just as people believed that they had delivered the letters addressed to the deceased soldiers. Even after this building was constructed, the trend continued and spread. Now, people come here to send letters to those they can no longer reach.

"Ask about our rates at the counter.

"I'd never heard of it," you concluded. I nodded and we both looked to the woman.

The woman said, "It`s five bucks to leave a letter."

"We're good," you said.

"So what's with the dogs?" I asked.

She cocked her eye at me and grunted. I lifted my eyes to the roof and repeated myself.

"No one loves a mailman more than a dog." She caught the skeptic look that passed between us and snorted. "If not, why are they always chasing after them?" With that she turned and shoved her way out the door and closed it behind her. We stood, hands in our pockets, looking around.

"What are we supposed to do here?" I asked.

"Read the letters?"

I was uncomfortable with the thought, but you squatted down and picked up a handful of crumpled papers. After a moment I joined you. The first letter I held was from a father to children he couldn't see due to a court ruling, at least from what I could gather. It ended pitifully. It ended with threats of suicide. The next was no better—a fiancé whose intended died in a car accident. I set it aside and picked up another, and after that, another. Some were detailed accounts of entire relationships. Among many there were common motifs, and I started to categorize them in my head. *High School Sweethearts Gone Sour, Soul Mates with Cancer, Friends and Fatal Accidents.*

The unifying theme of each was longing, of course. Maybe different shapes of longing, but longing of such pure intensity that it felt dirty just to touch the paper. A kind of longing I had forgotten was possible.

I looked to you once, but you had your back toward me.

I slipped outside while you were looking the other way, palmed the woman five dollars, and she gave me a sheet of paper and an envelope. I came back in and sat facing the wall, writing my own hurried letter. By the end of it, I was crying. You must have heard, because you asked if we should go, and when I didn't say anything you got up and maneuvered past me to push the door open and step outside. I stood up, scattering papers off the counter as I found my feet, and shoved my letter in the envelope, and the envelope in a cubby. You'd already made it to the front door by the time I caught up.

I followed you out past the woman, and down the road to your house.

That night we nursed our bottle and didn't talk much. We didn't meet each other's eyes. I felt the drip of each second reverberate in my bones until it was in my head beating. *Tick tick tick*, like the second hand of a clock.

I wanted to touch your face, but there was ink on my fingers.

There was something broken that passed from the letters into our bloodstream. I don't know why else I would have hesitated. I don't know why else you would have asked what you asked.

"Who?"

And I don't know why else I would have answered. I don't know why else my answer would have led to tears. I don't know why else my tears would have made you so angry.

And I don't know why else it would have come to fists, except maybe that's just how it is with love.

Remember the story of Bluebeard? The young girl he married. They lived in a great big house together, and everything was fine for a while. She was beautiful, he was doting. Maybe it wasn't love exactly, but it showed potential. And all he ever asked was that she never open this one door at the end of the main hall. But of course, she did what she ought not, and all that potential turned to so much ash in her mouth. So much blood on his hands.

That's what lovers are. A series of closed doors that ought not to be opened.

The next part was all bits, and pieces, and body parts really. A few times I went for the door, and I'd feel the knob in my hands, and then you'd pull me back. Sometimes you would go to leave, and I would bar the way. Sometimes I'd be pushing you. Sometimes your hands would be on my throat. And all the time there was a deluge flooding out of us. The deluge we had passed between each other's mouths. That we'd tasted on each other's tongues. But we had never asked about.

<3

Cinderella left a glass slipper behind, we all know that. Other lesser-known lovers left behind their fair share as well. My favorite, Allerleirauh, also known as She-Bear, or Many-Fur, or Donkey-Skin, left a golden reel, a golden spindle, and a golden ring. There have been leaves from the tree of everlasting life, apple sprigs stolen from gods, and talking horse heads all laid on the altar of love.

I had none of those things. Instead I left behind my socks and a few cigarette butts. My mucus on your collar. The imprint of my fingernails in your shoulder.

The sun didn't exactly rise that day due to the heavy blanket of storm clouds that had settled in during the early morning. When the rain fell, I found myself on the street somehow, two blocks away from your house, heading up the main road. The early risers were trickling into the street for work. Some drove by me slowly, and I could never figure out if it was because of the rain, which was coming down in sheets, or the light pattern of blood down my front. Regardless, none of them stopped.

Under their straps the dogs bucked with the wind, and I paused to watch. The rain beat against their plastic fur and slid down the tin roof and out of the storm drain harmlessly. My hair, my shirt, my everything was plastered tight to my bones in a way that made me feel stiff and heavy.

I could have walked on, but I no longer knew where I was going. So instead I climbed the ladder.

The wind is usually kind. It passes messages and whispers truths. In many stories, the wind carries lost things back to where they belong. Precious items to their homes just when they're needed most. Lovers back to the beloved. It may take a long time, and it may take a lot of switching of breezes, but isn't it always worth a shot to return back to where you were before?

To do something other than wait, watching the sky?

I'm not saying it was right, what I did, but I am saying that if you love something you should have the chance to chase it. Even if you're something plastic, and it's something dead.

The roof was slick. I unhooked the bungee cords from the side that I had climbed and crawled on all fours to each dog. I unwound them and set them down, then moved on to the next. When I was finished I finally looked back, but they'd done nothing but slide down the roof and get caught on the storm drain in a great heap. The wind would make them tremble every now and then, but it did nothing more.

I got to my feet and I took the nearest dog and threw it in the air. The draft caught it, and it spun upward. For a moment, maybe, I thought I could see it riding on the wind, nipping the heels of dead postmen. Then it crashed to the ground.

I took another, I threw it, and the wind did nothing but let it fall. And the next. And on. Until I was running out of chances, and then the chances were gone.

I climbed back down the ladder to the dogs. Several had been dented. Their bottoms were a great big hole, and rain poured into them. I picked one up and threw it back into the air, but it thumped against the roof and came tumbling back down. I tried in vain to wipe the water out of my eyes, but it kept coming.

If this were a fairy tale, I thought, if this were love, then this would be the moment when you would come, and you would find me. I would open my arms to you. We would pour into one another. You would take me somewhere warm and dry. We would tell each other the words that would make us human again.

    I sat down with the dogs. I held the closest one to my chest. I waited.

My Darling, Where Have You Gone?

Witch-Girl lived in a hut made out of tin-sheets smelted together, deep in the woods. There were no other people. Only animals. This was a forest of loss, and people can't handle loss as easily as animals and Witch-Girls. Even Witch-Girl could hardly handle it. She grew thinner day by day.

She'd already lost her own fair share by coming to the woods. She had no choice in coming. She was a Witch-Girl, and she belonged to these woods. She'd brought along a cabinet in which she kept things from her life before. From it, she had gone on losing.

She lost her mother's knitting needles when Bear had pulled out Otter's nails and Otter had needed something thin and sharp to pry open oysters with. Her father's lighter she lost to Tiger, when Bear had shaved him bald and he'd needed fires to keep him warm through winter. Her brother's kite she lost to Owl, when Bear had clipped his wings too short to fly.

Loss always happens. It is the nature of things to be lost. Witch-Girl knew this. She was ready and content to blink out of existence piece by piece alongside the keepsakes of her past. But Bear was a problem. He had thrown the timing all off.

Witch-Girl thought of this and laid on her bed, counting her ribs. She thought of this as she sat by the cabinet and counted her things. She could feel less ribs than she wanted. She had less things than she should. Soon, she thought, she would have to do something drastic.

Just as Witch-Girl was thinking this, Bear was waking in his cave to the gnawing. He shook dew off his coat and licked blood off his muzzle. The gnawing was never exactly hunger. It was never exactly loss. But it was always there, and each day it was always worse.

Bear only knew one way to quiet it.

Every animal in the forest knew Cat and Scorpion hated each other. Even though the woods were big enough that they could live in peace without ever having to see each other, they'd chosen dens no more than three feet apart. Cat wouldn't move, and neither would Scorpion. That's just how it is sometimes. Bear left his cave that morning and headed towards them. Along the way he picked up a rock and tested it between his jaws.

"Cat," He called, outside her den. "Come out."

"Why?" Cat answered from inside. Cat was usually had some sense, but somehow Scorpion always managed to make her lose it.

"I want to see your claws," Bear said. "I think they're the strongest in the forest."

"And why do you care about that," she asked.

"It's only that I heard Moose saying the other day that Scorpion's were stronger," Bear said.

Cat came out of her hole. "That's a lie," she said. "Look." She flexed out her paws, and from their pads emerged her nails, hard and white.

Bear sat down. "They do look stronger than Scorpion's could ever be," he said.

From the den across the way, Scorpion came scuttling, his claws raised above his head.

"Not true," he said. "Look. Just look." He raised them and gave each a snap.

"It's too bad there's no way to know for sure," Bear said. "Unless maybe..." Bear trailed off with a shrug.

"Maybe what?" Cat asked.

"Maybe if we had a contest," Bear said. He rolled the stone out between the two of them. "We can see who does the most damage to this rock."

To Bear, the rock was a little thing. Nearly nothing at all. Everything seemed like nearly nothing at all. But to Cat, it was larger than her own head, and to Scorpion, it was double the size of his body.

"This is a trap," Cat said.

"Well, if you're afraid to lose, I understand," Bear said. He took the rock up in his paw and shrugged.

Scorpion snapped his claws, and scuttled through the dirt. His mandibles clicked together as he laughed. "She is, she is, she is."

"I am not," Cat said.

"Then prove it," Bear said, setting the rock back down.

"You're so eager, you go first," Cat said.

Scorpion hesitated, but Bear gave him a nudge towards the rock and a small nod. He reared up and struck it with his tail. He crawled all over it, pinching, stinging, eventually bashing it with his claws and biting it. The rock stayed whole. But Scorpion fell apart. His tail bent until the tip chipped off. His claws cracked and split in two. By the end he was blood-soaked and broken.

He fell back wheezing. "It can't be broken," he said.

"By you," Cat said.

"Well it's your turn now. Let's see you do better," Scorpion said.

With a heave of her chest, Cat approached the rock. She circled it. Then she sprang on top of it. She clawed, and she bit. She did everything she could, everywhere she could. Her teeth shattered and her claws wrenched out of the pads of her feet.

She collapsed next to it, blood dripping from her mouth. The rock was fine.

"You did no better than me," Scorpion said.

"Shut up," Cat said. "I should have eaten you when I had the chance."

"And I should have stung you," Scorpion said. "I hate you. I hate you more than I've ever anything else."

"There's nothing you can do about it now," Bear said laughing. He stood and took the rock in his mouth and cracked it in two. "Or you could go and see the Witch-Girl, I guess."

Bear walked away, still laughing, the gnawing in his gut quieted, but still there.

Witch-Girl wasn't quite young. And she wasn't quite old. She had been caught in between for almost as long as she could remember. She felt caught in between too much. In between being and not being. In between having and losing. In between sense and nonsense.

She wanted to go either one way or the other. She knew she could never be young again, so she supposed it would be better being old. Being old at least meant she would have more sense, and having sense was what Witch-Girls were supposed to do.

The animals came to her for sense. They thought sense meant solving their problems. Witch-Girl thought it meant learning to live with them. But the animals insisted on their way, so Witch-Girl did what she could.

Cat and Scorpion dragged themselves to her tin cottage after Bear left them. Cat went to her front door, Scorpion to the back. When she heard them knocking, Witch-Girl checked out her windows and saw them bleeding. She felt like turning them away. But she had never turned anyone away.

She let Cat in, then carried Scorpion to the bed. Small things had trouble navigating her house even when whole. The floors were covered in lost things. Some unimportant, like buttons, socks, lighters. Others, more dear. Single pages of long, honest letters. Pocket watches with engraved insides. The last bits of love that burned the brightest before vanishing completely. Lost things were always finding their way to the Witch-Girl. But she couldn't give these to anyone. She had to wait until they were found.

When Cat and Scorpion were settled on her bed she looked them over.

"What seems to be the problem?" she asked. Witch-Girl always asked. She never assumed.

"Look at us," Scorpion said. "My claws and tail are broken."

"My teeth, my claws," Cat lisped.

Witch-Girl nodded. "I see," she said. "Have you tried accepting that they're gone?"

Cat hissed and raised her back as much as she could. Witch-Girl sighed and went to her cabinet.

"Even things you never thought were dear to you can be things that hurt when you lose them. And when you do lose them, they may not be able to be replaced," Witch-Girl said.

"What's your point?" Scorpion asked.

"I just want you to be sure," Witch-Girl said.

"We are," Cat said.

Witch-Girl reached into the cabinet to the way back. She took out her mother's glass rose and held it in the light so it cast rainbows against her wall. She tried to think of what she lost of her mother and couldn't. She thought of what she still had; that her mother loved colors, that she had painted pictures of their garden, of flowers, of woods that were like these but also not at all. Then Witch-Girl brushed the lost clutter off of her table and laid the rose down. She took a hammer to it.

"Come here," she said to Cat.

When she was done, Cat had glass teeth and glass claws, Scorpion a glass tail and pincers. They were jagged, but they worked. She placed them outside her back door.

"Loss can be overcome, if you have someone else who—" Witch-Girl started. Cat bit into Scorpion's neck and Scorpion buried his tail between Cat's eyes. They both fell down dead on Witch-Girl's doorstep.

She looked at them for a moment, the sun sparkling against the bloodied glass. She went inside her house and came back out a moment later, dressed in a cloak and carrying a bear trap under her arm. She headed to the river.

The trick with Cat and Scorpion only gave Bear the slightest relief. Not long after he felt the gnawing worse than ever. He thought of eating, which could sometimes calm it. He thought of blood, which almost always did.

And then Bear saw Dog, bounding between trees, sniffing and wagging his tail.

"Here, boy," Bear called. Dog raised a cocked head. "Come here," Bear called again. Dog came bounding.

Witch-Girl set the trap under the leaves along the bank of the river. She hated being out. She hated feeling the sun filter through the trees and land on her skin. She hated seeing a place that was very nearly but never quite the place she had come from. It hurt. But she couldn't put it off any longer. Something had to be done about Bear, regardless of the price.

Bear had intended to eat Dog in some way that would be both clever and surprising. He had walked with Dog for some time, trying to piece together how. But while they walked Bear had been distracted. Dog was amiable. Maybe the most amiable animal in the forest. And there were very few animals that would talk to Bear.

Without realizing it, Bear had forgotten to plan. Forgotten even the gnawing.

"It's a nice day," Dog had said. Bear found himself agreeing. "What should we do?" Dog asked.

"Let's take a walk," Bear said.

Dog's tail wagged. "Where?" He asked.

"Down by the river," Bear said. "We can try to catch some fish." He no longer felt, at the moment, like eating Dog at all.

Dog bounded around Bear as they walked. Forward and back, in circles. Tail wagging and ears up. For Dog, walking with Bear felt like the time before he'd come to the woods. When he had a bed inside, a collar around his neck, and someone to keep his fur clean, to walk near him, and to tell him what to do. Dog didn't think Bear was bad, like most of the other animals said. Dog didn't think anyone was bad. It wasn't in his nature to.

Bear picked a stick up off the ground and threw. Dog ran after it and brought it back. Bear picked it up and threw it again. They passed the time this way as they walked, Bear watching the simple ease with which Dog ran, the simple joy on Dog's face, and feeling no gnawing or need. Bear threw the stick, and Dog ran after it.

Then Dog let out a yelp and fell to the ground in a heap, trembling. Bear smelled fresh blood in the air. His stomach blossomed with pain and want.

"Dog, are you alright?" Bear called.

"I think I'm hurt," Dog said. "Could you come help me?"

"I don't think I should," Bear said. "I don't know how."

"Please," Dog said.

Bear came closer to Dog. Each step the blood smell was stronger. He could smell torn, fresh meat. Each step the gnawing in Bear grew. He looked at Dog, and saw the trap tearing through his hind leg.

"It's bad," Bear said. "You'd better go see the Witch-Girl."

"I don't think I can move," Dog said. "Can you go get her?" Bear shook his head. Witch-Girl and Bear had as little to do with each other as sense and nonsense.

"You have to do something, then," Dog said. "Please."

"Alright," Bear said. "I'll try." First he knocked Dog out with a blow to the head, and then he clipped off Dog's wounded leg. He broke the tip off one of his claws and took one of his long hairs and sewed the base shut into a nub. He woke Dog with a shake.

Dog got up on his three legs and took a few wobbling steps. He looked at Bear without the joy from before, but also without pain.

"I think this will be alright," Dog said. But Bear could only remember Dog the way Dog had been, easy, bounding, and smiling. This Dog wasn't the same.

"No," Bear said. "You're all wobbly. Let me try again."

He knocked Dog out and clipped a little of his whole hind leg off. He sewed some of this to the nub. Then he clipped the paw off the mangled leg and sewed that to the end of the other. He woke Dog and Dog stood up, but now his ass end drooped towards the ground and dragged behind him.

"I can live with this, I guess," Dog said.

"No, now it's all uneven," Bear said. "Let me try again."

Again, he knocked Dog out. He clipped the front legs. He nibbled some off. He sewed. But the lengths were always off. He cut more. He ate more. He sewed. It was never right. It was never the same as it had been.

Soon Dog was nothing more than four paws sewed to the base of his body. He wiggled on the ground and looked up at Bear.

"This is worse than before," Dog said. "Now I have to inch along like a worm."

Bear felt the gnawing course through him in great waves. He wanted to pick Dog up and swallow him whole. He nearly did, but when he closed his eyes he remembered how Dog had looked him in the eyes and wagged his tail.

"Well, I've done all I can do. Besides, it's not my problem. Not my fault. I didn't have to help, you know," Bear said.

"I should have known better than to trust you," Dog said. "I should've gone to the Witch-Girl."

Bear raised a paw and Dog flinched back. Pain stabbed through Bear's belly. He stood up and lumbered away from the Dog.

"Why don't you, then?" Bear said. "It has nothing to do with me."

It took Dog all day to reach the Witch-Girl's hut. By the time he got there, it was dusk. He scratched at the front door, and Witch-Girl opened it and took him in her arms. She laid him on the bed where Cat and Scorpion had sat.

"What seems to be the problem?" she asked.

"I have no legs," Dog said. "They got caught in a trap. Bear tried to set it right, but he couldn't."

Witch-Girl's hand went to her mouth and she nipped the skin between her thumb and index finger. When she pulled her hand away it glistened with spittle. "A trap," she said.

"Yes," Dog said. "Please say you can help."

"Have you tried just accepting that they're gone?"

"I did at first, but then it got worse. I don't think I can live like this," he said. He looked at her with begging eyes. The kind of eyes that Dog does best.

Witch-Girl went to the cabinet. She had to reach way back, till her last rib was inside. She took out her father and brother's walking sticks. She could remember very little of them. Except that they were tall, and they walked with a sense of ease. She laid the sticks across her table and picked up a saw.

"Somethings we lose aren't easily replaced," she said.

"What?" Dog asked.

"I'm just asking if you're sure," she said, looking at him. He was. She set to sawing the walking sticks in half. She took them to the bed where Dog lay quivering.

"Knock me out first," Dog asked. "I don't want to feel the pain."

"It would just be waiting for you when you woke up," Witch-Girl said.

"Bear knocked me out," Dog said. "Please."

"I'm not Bear," Witch-Girl said. She set to work undoing Bear's stitches. She grafted the sticks one after another in Dog's empty sockets, and all the while he yelped and whined. When she was finished she capped off the sticks with his old paws.

He got to his feet and took a few steps.

"I used to be able to bound," Dog said. "Now I move so stiffly."

"Sometimes after loss, life is a little stiffer," Witch-Girl said. "You'll get used to it."

Dog left, his tail and head still drooped. Witch-Girl was used to this. Making sense didn't mean making people happy. She laid back on her bed, closed her eyes, and felt her father and brother dissolving.

The gnawing was worse than it'd ever been. Just the thought of Dog, all paw and no leg, caused it to flare up like millions of tiny teeth trying to chew their way out from beneath his skin. He didn't want to think about Dog. He didn't know why he did. It wasn't his problem, or his pain, and so it was none of his business. But his mind insisted. It kept insisting. Then it started insisting about others. Cat and Scorpion broken to bits. Deer running from him, bleeding from his bite in her haunches. Bird's feathers plucked and scattered across his den.

None of these were his problems, he thought.

But all of these were his fault, the gnawing answered.

He would do anything to make it stop. But every time he quieted it, it came back worse. He couldn't go to Witch-Girl, the thought alone made him want to tether the ground between his claws. Besides, she'd never see him. But there were other options for sense in the woods. A different kind of sense. But sense nonetheless.

Such as Turtle, who lived deep in the marsh, where the mud was thick and black, and the fewest animals stayed. Bear made his way towards her, and each step he took the hole in his belly grew larger. Ached more.

It was midnight by the time he found the marsh and started wading through the thick mud. It caked his fur, first only up to his knees. But then up to his belly. After a while he had to hold his snout up so he could breathe. Then he saw Turtle's massive back rising like a hill out of the muck, and her two, large yellowed eyes.

"Turtle, I've come for help," Bear said. She was one of the only animals Bear had to look up to in the forest. Only one of the few animals larger than bear. She was as tall as Bear's cave, and double the length of Bear himself.

Turtle looked at him, blinking slowly, and her limbs crept back into her shell. First her legs, one by one, then her long neck and head, until all she was was a dark cave.

"Go away, Bear. Even I've heard all about you," Turtle said.

"I'm in pain. I think I'm dying," he said.

"You can't expect others to stick their necks out for you when you have a reputation for biting off heads," Turtle said.

"Please," Bear said. Turtle said nothing back.

"Please," Bear tried again, and nothing came again. The gnawing was a jackhammer in his guts. He felt the seam of himself ready to split open. He did what was in his nature to do. He took a rock up from under the water and stood on his hind legs with it lifted over his head.

"Just help me, Turtle," Bear said. "Don't make me do this." But Turtle wouldn't budge.

Bear leapt upon her shell and began to beat her with the rock. With each blow the gnawing subsided, then roared back to life. Bear struck again, and again. Until a crack formed in Turtle's shell. Then it grew. Then it started to split open. Turtle finally came out, screaming. A leg shot out, and knocked Bear off into the water. He struck his head on a rock, and floated there, unconscious.

Turtle dragged herself forward through the swamp, leaving Bear behind, and heading for the Witch-Girl.

Witch-Girl didn't sleep so much as drift. Off to other places and times, or more often than not, to nowhere. Just white space stretching on forever. Before, when she first came to the woods, she would find herself drifting back home—to the place where her mother, father, and brother still lived She would watch them do what they always had done, unable to be seen, or heard, or touched and comforted. In the early days they were as vivid as she was plump and solid. But piece by piece, bits of them fell away until her mother had no face. Her brother's hair lost its color. Her father's voice warped into static. Finally they were just smears of color, suggestions of people, and nothing more. This was worse than the white ache of nothing.

It was to the not-home home that she'd gone when Dog left.

She had watched the color swatches sitting at their table, moving in ways that were almost familiar, hearing muffled voices echo at her, as if she were submerged in water. Then she was pulled back out by the earth quaking. *The woods are falling apart*, she thought. She was on her feet before the world she lived in had clearly taken shape, making her way to the window and staring out it with a rare smile on her face.

Outside, the night was clear and the woods were whole. But the ground shook again. A swatch of trees bent forward and snapped. Turtle was coming, hers eyes rolled back in her head and foam coating her beak, parting the trees like long grass. Turtle's shell was coming off her back in huge chunks and tumbling to the ground. Witch-Girl ran out of her shack to meet her.

"Bear's killed me. He's killed me. Quick, help," Turtle said, dragging herself to a stop near the Witch-Girl's backdoor.

"Wha—" Witch-Girl started to ask, but Turtle let out one long, whistling scream. Witch-Girl turned back around and stepped over the bodies of Cat and Scorpion into her house. She reached inside her cabinet, all the way back. She had to climb in to search the dark corners. But it was no use. Only Witch-Girl was in the cabinet, and nothing more.

She came back out. "I don't have anything for you. I'm sorry," she said.

"Give me your home," Turtle said. "It'll do."

"But it's all I have," Witch-Girl said.

"And my life is all I have," Turtle replied. "It's such a shabby home. But it'll be the perfect shell."

"Even if you don't think you love something, it still hurts to lose it," Witch-Girl said.

"You can build a new one," Turtle said.

"Sometimes a lost thing can't truly be replaced," Witch-Girl said.

"I'll lose my life if you don't give me your home," Turtle said.

"But you've had your life for such a long time, and I've only had my home for a short time," Witch-Girl said.

"And doesn't time make something much more dear?" Turtle asked.

Witch-Girl felt her insides crumple, hollow and weak as a used-up tin can. She had no pieces of home left. She had no self left. She had no sense left.

"I don't know," she said. "I don't know because I've never been allowed to have anything for very long."

"Give me your home, and I'll give you some sense you can keep forever," Turtle said. Witch-Girl looked up at her. At the torn, exposed muscle under her shell. At her yellow, crusted eyes reflecting Witch-Girl back at herself, neither young nor old, nor wise or dumb, nor here or there. Just something temporary on its way to being nothing.

"Okay," Witch-Girl said. "Take it."

Turtle shook the last of her shell off and in a blink of an eye stuffed herself into the tin hut. She popped her legs out the windows, her head and tail through the doors. She stood, pulling the tin sheets out of the ground with one quick tearing sound.

"Seal it up," Turtle said.

"Give me the sense," Witch-Girl said.

"After."

So Witch-Girl went round, beating the tin into Turtle's stomach plate until it was fixed tight. When it was finished, Turtle looked her over with an expression somewhere between pity and disgust.

"This is the greatest bit of sense you'll ever hear, so listen carefully," Turtle said. Witch-Girl listened, her hands held out before her as if she could catch Turtle's words and keep them forever, even if most things aren't meant to be kept.

"Other people's problems are the problems of other people," Turtle said. Then she started on her way home, Witch-Girl's hut rocking on her back, spilling out bits of splintered wood, lost lighters, and crumpled pages of love letters and grocery lists.

Witch-Girl watched her go, breath hitching in her shallow chest. When Turtle was no more than a speck, Witch-Girl dropped down to her knees next to Cat and Scorpion.

"What the fuck?" she asked.

Bear woke in the marsh and felt the gnawing ripping open his ribs. He got to his feet, and having nowhere to go, followed the trail of Turtle's body through the marsh and woods.

Witch-Girl had no home. She looked around at the floor, cluttered with broken lost things, and her bed, split in half, and having nowhere to go, walked towards anywhere else.

At the river, the Witch-Girl and the Bear met for the first time since the Witch-Girl first arrived, and all the animals had been present to welcome her. That was either a not-so-long time ago, or a not-very-short time ago. Bear couldn't remember, and neither could the Witch-Girl. Bear thought Witch-Girl looked thinner. She looked like she had dissolved. Witch-Girl thought Bear looked bloated. Like a balloon on the edge of bursting.

Witch-Girl finished her look at Bear and dropped down to sit on the bank of the river. Bear came to sit next to her.

"Witch-Girl, I need your help," he said.

"Other people's problems are the problems of other people," she said. "Go away."

"You smell like dying, Witch-Girl. What are you doing out of your home?" Bear asked.

"Turtle took it after you wrecked her shell. I have nothing now, and it's all your fault," Witch-Girl said.

"So I am your problem, and not someone else's," Bear said. He laid his head on her lap and Witch-Girl felt the mud of the marsh ooze out of his fur and through her clothes to chill her belly.

"Cat and Scorpion are dead. After you tricked them, I replaced the broken bits with glass and they sunk that glass deep into each other," Witch-Girl said and wound her fingers in Bear's fur.

"Then it was you who killed them by giving," Bear said. "And it had nothing to do with me."

"I was only fixing," Witch-Girl said, pulling Bear's hair.

"Well, what did it fix?" Bear growled. He lifted his head up so they were looking eye to eye. "At least they had each other, Witch-Girl. Who do I have? No one. Not even Dog."

"You ate all of his legs," Witch-Girl said.

"But you set the trap," Bear said.

"It was for you. Because all you do is destroy. All you do is take," Witch-Girl said.

"I can't help it, Witch-Girl." Bear put his face close to hers and bared his teeth so she could see herself reflected in them; a dozen thinning blurs of a once-girl. "There is a gnawing inside of me. I'm hungry, Witch-Girl, so hungry."

"Hunger's no excuse," Witch-Girl said.

"And how would you know? Why aren't you hungry? You're all alone, too. Why don't you feel it?" Bear asked.

"I never said I didn't," Witch-Girl said, taking one of Bear's long teeth in her hand and running her thumb over it.

"Do you want to see it?" Bear asked. Witch-Girl nodded and let go of his tooth.

Bear rose up to his hind legs and stood before her. He touched a claw to his belly and it split open as if along a seam. He opened his insides to her. Witch-Girl saw his ribs, heart, lungs and blood. And behind it all, she saw the gnawing. Witch-Girl reached her arms into Bear. She reached way back, further than she could go, until her feet slipped inside, and she was snug among his organs. She took the gnawing in her lap.

"Does it hurt?" Witch-Girl asked.

"Stay there," Bear said.

With one long hair the Bear sewed himself back up with Witch-Girl inside. He dropped down to his feet and walked. He walked far enough that he reached the end of the woods, and then he walked on. He walked so long that Witch-Girl slipped into his tissue, his bone, and blood until she was as much Bear as Witch or Girl. Now in the woods, there is no Witch-Girl. No hut filled with lost things. No place for you to go when you need to search for something dear. It's gone, now. Into the belly of the Bear.

Thursday

After your rejection, I'll start drinking. Or rather, I'll keep drinking, but I'll be doing it with intent. That's a beast of a completely different color. I'll become a beast of a completely different color. By Thursday, you won't recognize me.

I'll be on my way back from the store with a clutch of forties in a plastic bag when Old Suede Hat will fall into step next to me. His five o'clock shadow is burnt rubber. His eyes are the last embers of a funeral pyre. Still, I'll tell him I'm not interested, that's how hung up on you I'll still be.

"Hush," Old Suede Hat'll say, stepping in front of me, his hands cupped closed in front of my face. "I have something special for you. But you have to be brave. Can you be brave, child?" I'll shrug and crack open a forty. Old Suede Hat'll open his hands anyway, and inside there'll be a cockroach waving his antennae.

"This little fellow would like to invite you to a wedding tonight, and everyone knows you're in no position to refuse."

By that point my heartache will be public domain, parodied in the yowls of street cats. Anyway, it's impossible to refuse Old Suede Hat anything. Which is why I hate him, and sometimes why I want him, too. But if I have you, I could refuse him easy as breathing. Even without you, I'll still try.

"It won't work out," I'll say.

"It doesn't have to work out to be a good time," Old Suede Hat will say, winking.

"I'm too big."

"Come on now, quit lying. We both know you're as small as an ant. Why, honey, I can hardly see you."

By the time I lower the forty from my lips, it'll be true. Or maybe it's already true. It feels true. But regardless, when I lower the forty, I'll find myself tucked in Old Suede Hat's hands with the cockroach, my clothes in a heap on the ground. Old Suede Hat will run his thumb over my naked body. I'll feel every bit of grit. It'll be like sandpaper.

"I've got a little doll's dress for you to wear, sweetie. Old Suede Hat's not going to send you out looking so sad and sloppy."

It'll be pink. Frilled. Childish. Not even Barbie would wear it. She'd have passed it on to Stacy years ago. After he's dressed me, Old Suede Hat will put me and the cockroach down on the ground near a thimble.

"Get in, and I'll pull you along," the roach will say. I'll hesitate, knowing that for every kindness, I'll be expected to show a specific kindness in return. That's why I gave you that ring, you know. But I'd forgotten it only works one way. Old Suede Hat made me forget. Sometimes he follows that rule, like he's a woman. If you followed it, we wouldn't be having this conversation, and on Thursday, I wouldn't end up in a thimble wearing a pink plastic party dress, begging Old Suede Hat for my forties.

"There will be plenty to drink at the party," Old Suede Hat'll say. "Have fun, kids." The cockroach will scurry along, dragging me behind, till we come to a crack in an old church wall where the wedding will be.

When we get inside and still haven't spoken, he'll try to ease the tension by making small talk. He'll say: "Look how festive it is. They've decorated nicely." The hall will be smeared with bacon grease. They'll have sunk lightning bugs in it head-first so the glow of their asses will light the way. It'll remind me of your morning breath and your mourning eyes. I'll tell him it's beautiful to be polite, and we won't have anything more to talk about.

The hall will already be full. Cockroaches will be dressed up in fine rags, antennae tucked under bottle-caps and twist-tie headbands. While we find our seats, my date will touch his many hands to mine and tell me I'm the most beautiful woman there. Even more beautiful than the bride. She and the groom will be sucking face at the altar in a way I won't be able to watch.

You kissed me like that once. Do you remember?

After the vows, we'll clear the chairs from the floor and the band will start sawing their limbs together. There'll be a grasshopper fiddling. He'll be the only one who isn't a cockroach other than me, and he'll avoid my eyes the whole time. A buffet of refuse will be wheeled in. My date will bring me something strong and bitter to drink, and it'll turn my head. Or maybe it'll be because of the way he whirls me around on the dance floor. Over and over. Until I'm falling against his chest, pinned by the cage of his many arms. He'll draw my face close and run his antenna down my cheek.

"You belong here, sweetie," he'll say. "With me." The music will swell, and I won't notice the smell so much anymore. I'll start thinking it's true. I'll give up then, and let him place his mandibles on my mouth. You won't disappear from my mind, but I'll know for sure you'll never be possible again. Not after I've kissed the roach. And in a way this will be worse than hoping, but maybe also better.

And that's how just how it'll be. But, darling, you could stop it all with a single word. You know you could.

Please?

Ten Things I'm Irrationally Afraid of (Listed in No Particular Order)

I'm afraid to sleep on the ground floor. I'm sure one night I'll wake up and someone will be standing outside of the window looking in. Actually, if I'm being honest, I'm afraid of this for all floors, and the higher it is, the worse it will be when it happens.

I'm always afraid I'm forgetting something important, but never afraid enough to turn off the T.V. and think about it. If I'm being honest, it's because I'm afraid of what I might remember. But if I'm being really honest, it's because I'm afraid that if I try, I'll find out it's already gone forever. But if I'm being really, really honest, it's because I'm also just lazy.

I'm afraid one day I'll consume human flesh. On accident, of course. I'm convinced this happens more often than we think. That it's a big secret we just collectively don't talk about. Sometimes, I'm sure it's already happened. There's no real way for me to know.

I'm afraid to know.

I'm afraid I'll end up alone. Not in the romantic sense. I don't think that's very particular or that irrational. I mean alone in the middle of the ocean, drowning. Below me there'll be a shadow in the water, very large and very tentacled. Rising.

I'm 73% certain that I'll end up getting my foot caught in a bear trap, though I've never lived anywhere near bears. It just seems like the kind of thing that would happen to me.

I'm afraid that I'll end up one of those people who spends the last few years of their life sitting in a McDonald's dining room at the break of dawn, drinking Styrofoam cup after Styrofoam cup of coffee, talking about football, and how there will never be an invention that comes along and replaces a good old-fashioned broom and dust pan.

There are nights where there is nothing you can say or do that'll convince me that there is not a cockroach living in my ear.

I'm afraid that I'll breathe too hard, and my septum ring will come loose, and lodge itself in my brain. I mean you never know. It could happen. At the very least it makes more sense than the bear trap thing.

I'm afraid that one night I'll be pursued by a pack of stray dogs. It'll be dark, and cold, and there will be no lights on in the nearby windows. While I'm running, my kneecaps will detach, and I'll fall.

In the pack there will be one dog that stands out. A pug in a hand-knit sweater that used to be nice. It'll say "Mama's Lil All Star Barker." That'll be what hurts the most. Not the sinking of tiny teeth into the bridge of my nose, or the shifting bones in my knees.

But the fact that he had been loved, once. And it hadn't been enough.

I'LL TELL YOU A LOVE STORY

Wolf's Wake

The Queen of All Magic lived in a studio apartment on Fifth Ave. Last time I went to see her she was looking a little worn around the eyes. "Baby doll," she said, "bring me some aspirin." So I did.

Her bathtub was always full to the brim with water murky as the bayou, complete with big fat lily pads big as my head floating in the water. Underneath, there were scaled creatures sliding around on top of each other, mouths puckering at the surface asking for something to eat. Sometimes they were long, black bass, and sometimes they were fat, speckled goldfish, but always they were hungry. The aspirin was in the medicine cabinet behind the belladonna and the milkweed. She took two with a shot of bourbon. The Queen of All Magic didn't have any couches or chairs. She was sitting on the floor next to a low table, all the lights dimmed, but not so much that I couldn't see her clear as day.

"You been crying?" I asked her, and she looked at me from under heavy lids and blinked really slow. "'Cause of what happened?"

"And what do you know about what happened?" she said, pouring more bourbon in her cup. I shared blood with The Queen of All Magic. Everyone does in some small way, which means everyone also shares blood with each other. They just forget that sometimes, Queen said. But me and Queen's blood was weaved together tight. My great-grandmother was her sister.

"I know Wolf is dead," I said, putting my hands in the pockets of my overalls and looking up at the carpet hanging on her wall. It was a heavy one, showing all the faces of the moon man knows, and behind them some of the secret ones men could just guess at. Queen knew them all by name, and she'd teach 'em to me by whispering 'em in my ear at night when I slept.

"Yeah, he's dead alright," Queen said, her voice steady as iron. "Got his brains blown out huffing and puffing around the wrong hussy's house." She sipped her bourbon, and fished a cigarette out of the pack on her table. She stared at the wall for a long time before tucking it in her mouth and lighting it.

Sometimes Queen and Wolf ran around together, and sometimes they didn't. 'Times they were tight as the sun and the moon, laughing and playing with the universe together. Other times they were at each other's throats, Wolf going too far and Queen having to mop up after him. Always, though, they loved each other in their way. They were each other's everything, even when they were fooling around with somebody else, which was more often than not. The Queen of All Magic was like a flower you'd find deep in a marsh, barbed but beautiful too. You never knew if touching her would end up getting you poisoned, but you had to do it anyway. And Wolf was the handsomest man in town, in his own crooked way.

"You gonna fix it?" I asked.

"Ain't nothing left to fix this time," Queen said, blowing smoke out of her nose. It gathered in the air just above her head, and I saw inside it the shape of the universe folding in on itself, everything and everyone coming to a close.

"You mean that?" I asked, tilting my head at her and slitting my eyes. Sometimes Queen didn't fix things 'cause she thought they ought not be fixed. Like my marks at school, and the poorness of the people on the streets. She said we had to fix 'em ourselves with our own hands.

"There's only so much magic," she'd tell me, "and I can't go wasting it on every little thing."

I'd tell her that my bad marks were half her fault, 'cause she's the one who taught me all I knew. Like the time I put down on a history test that people, just like all the continents, were one big thing until slowly we all started to erode and drift away from one another. The teacher said it wasn't time for poetry. Queen just laughed when I told her.

Other times she didn't fix things because they couldn't be fixed, like when my Mama got cancer the second time, and we all just had to stand by and watch her wither. I near hated Queen then, but Grandma made me see reason after some time.

"I mean it," the Queen of All Magic said, her voice dropping like a brick. "The next time I see that dirty bastard will be when our skeletons are dancing together in the next life." She swilled the rest of her bourbon down and stubbed out her cigarette. She reached down the front of her dress and pulled out a stack of bills.

"Run on down to the store and buy us some party favors," said Queen. "Get everyone together at the usual spot. I feel like celebrating."

I took the money, but I could spot the lie. I was young but not an idiot. Sometimes adults mix those two things up. Even the Queen of All Magic, who usually knew better.

"What do you want?" I asked her, and she gave me a list.

First, I stopped at the corner store and passed him Queen's note with all the liquor she asked for. He looked it over then looked down his nose at me. He was an old guy. One of the ones who could remember Queen in her prime. Back then, I'd been told, puddles used to part so she could pass through, and the rain only fell when she said so. Her and Wolf could go out drinking and hit every bar without having to pay a single dime.

"She taking Wolf's death okay?" asked the old man. There was concern in his voice, and maybe a little jealousy, and longing too. Maybe, I thought, he was one of Queen's run-around dudes back in the day. They always wore their age a little different. Kept something like a star twinkling right behind their eyes. I looked for one in his, but he darted his eyes down, and scanned the list.

"Tell her I'll have it to her by eight. Tell her it's on the house," he said, pocketing the paper and turning away.

Next, I went to the grocer, and ordered the meat. Along the way I stopped and told this person and that, lounging on their steps, or walking down the street, about the party.

"Queen's having a get together," I'd tell 'em, and they'd stop whatever they were doing and do a double take.

"Tonight?" they'd say, and I'd nod. With each person I told the excitement built a little bit more in the air, till the whole neighborhood was buzzing. By the time I got to the Grocer the news had already gotten ahead of me. I'd stop to tell someone, but they'd cut me off, asking if it were true. All I had to do eventually was nod my head.

At the Grocer's I ordered the ribs, and the beef, and the fish. It was the most I had ever seen Queen order, but the Grocer didn't seem surprised. He just wrote 'em all down with a little nod of his head like this was business as usual. At the end he smiled, gave me a sucker for free, and pinched my cheek.

"You sure do look like Queen when she was young," he said.

"You ain't never seen her young," I said back. "Anyone who did is already dead."

He laughed and shook his head. "She's always young. Or at least, she look young enough. Now go on, and get out of here. I'll see you at the party."

I unwrapped the sucker and stuck it in my mouth. Tripped on out of the store grinning, forgetting for just a minute that Wolf was dead. Parties will do that to you. For a moment everything is weightless, and everyone is alive and laughing.

How I heard it told is like this: Queen and Wolf were the only two babies born on the day, years and years ago, that the moon and the sun blocked each other out twice. Wolf was born during that first eclipse in the morning, when the moon drifted over the sun and sat there for one straight hour like she was never gonna move. Then, that night right before the stroke of twelve, Queen was born when the sun came back and got his revenge. People said they knew right then and there they were a special pair. More than lovers, more than brothers and sisters, more than any blood could ever be, they were tied at the soul. There were sixteen hours between their births, and they always celebrated 'em together with one long party going from nine in the morning to twelve at night.

Then they'd stumble off together drunk as skunks, no matter if they were running around together or with some other folk. That's just how it was. People understood, even if sometimes they were a little jealous. Queenie and Wolf, they were two sides of one coin.

Until Wolf died that morning in some girl's bed. Her and her husband weren't from around here. They were new. Guess they didn't understand the score like we do. That putting a bullet through Wolf's head was like blowing apart one of the last halves of the magic and rightness in the world.

It wasn't exactly the first time he had died, but it was the last.

The party was held near the peat bogs, one of Queen's favorite places, where you can't tell for sure if you're stepping on solid ground or if it'll give way at any moment and you'll go tumbling down into the wet swamp. People came with lawn chairs and coolers, and barbeques were lined up to make one great train where folks took turns cooking the meat and wandering off to get drunk.

The whole ward was there, even the girl Wolf had been in bed with when he got his head shot off. Everyone got real quiet when she showed up, her eyes puffy and her nose red, but Queen walked up to her, put an arm around her, and offered her a plate of sloppy ribs. Everyone relaxed when the girl sunk her teeth in to 'em, and then laughed when she asked if we were sure it was safe, partying on the wetlands.

"Sure it's safe, honey," one of the men said, "so long as you watch out for gators."

Everyone laughed again, and the girl ducked her head, not sure if she was being made fun of or if she was supposed to laugh along.

"Clarence, you fool, don't you go spooking the poor thing," Queen said, batting the air with her hand and shooting him daggers. "She been through enough today. It's safe as houses, dear. Just watch where you put your feet and don't go to close to the edge." Queen gave her shoulder a squeeze and moved off through the crowd. I made my way across the soggy earth to her and cocked my eyebrows, asking what she was up to.

"Poor thing don't have any kin now that the cops snagged up her husband," Queen said, piling some chicken onto a paper plate, and shoving it into my hands. "So don't give me that look. Ain't her fault in the end. Wolf reaps what Wolf sows, and ain't a woman alive with any sense that woulda turned him down, married or not." A soft smile came to Queen's face. She already looked younger than she was, but somehow she managed to drop ten more years when she smiled like that. And she only smiled like that when she thought of Wolf. Or me, I guess. "Let's sit down and eat together, precious, and talk about how life is hanging."

And so we did. For a good half hour of the party Queen sat with me and listened to just me, which is a real honor. And 'cause she was listening, other people did too, until everyone there was asking me questions about my last test, or where I got my shoes, or what I did to my hair. Queen could do that. Pluck you up and make you a star. Redirect all her light your way so you could feel what it's like to be that warm.

That's probably how Wolf made that girl feel. Good enough that she forgot all the little details of her life were just that: little.

Not long after everybody was feeling good, drunk or not. The sun started setting and people started lighting lanterns, and hanging 'em up so all around the bog it looked like fairies were floating just above the water, darting in and out of the trees. People started playing music, dancing, and telling stories.

"Remember that time Wolf won all the money on that gambling boat? Even won the boat, too? Queen found out he'd cheated it right out from under everyone's noses. So when he went to sleep off his drunk on his new boat, she sunk it. He woke up just in time. Said he opened his eyes 'cause he thought he wet the bed, and instead finds he's waist deep in water, and all his winnings are, too"

"Remember when Wolf swam the river in the winter just to prove he could? And he got so cold he died of pneumonia right after?"

"It was to win back Queenie wasn't it? From some big city fella who said he was in the Olympics?"

"And it worked, too. She kissed his fool ass back to life."

"That's not how it went, is it? It was the city cat that swam the river and died, right?"

Queen just smiled at their stories. Never told them herself or changed 'em. She let them rewrite them as they pleased. Stories, she told me, have lives of their own. The teller and the listener give 'em their own meaning, so when they're being told what's really being said says more about whose saying it and whose hearing it than it does about the people in the story. Even when it's about you. All the stories were about Wolf, and since they were about Wolf, they were mostly also about Queen. But I also knew they were about us. All of us there.

Soon Queen got up after she'd listened to enough stories about Wolf and she started dancing. She danced beautiful, weaving in and out of the other dancers and taking whoever's hands she pleased. She danced with everyone there. Even the girl who'd seen

Wolf died. I stood up and danced with her once or twice, and she lifted me in the air and spun me around.

"I love you, little girl," she said. She didn't say it often. She didn't have to. But it felt good hearing it. Then she set me down.

By this point everyone was drunk or falling asleep on their feet, or both, so it's never told clearly. I know Queen would say that's alright. That they're just telling it the way it is for them. The most popular story, the one that makes the most sense to people now and got run in the paper, is that she fell into the water sometime around midnight, and she was so drunk she drowned. That's the one that would be true if she weren't the Queen of all Magic. Another, and this is the one the locals tell, is that she got snapped up by a big white gator that was waiting in the water just for her. They saw it rear up and take her in its mighty jaws.

But this is my story, and I know what the truth is 'cause I watched it. I had my eyes right on Queen and could see her clear as day as always. She was dancing further and further away from everyone, out towards the water. When she got to the very edge the surface of it rippled, and out came a big white head, and then shoulders, and then arms and legs, until a skeleton was standing atop the bog. It was Wolf. I could tell cause of the cap he had set on his head. He always wore it tilted just so. Queen took his hand and he spun her round and off they danced onto the water. I had made my way right to where Queen was standing when he swooped her off, and I alone watched. Everyone else was laughing and drinking, and too caught up in their own fun.

As they danced I saw Wolf rebuild himself piece after piece until he was all flesh. I thought then that they would head back to us, yell surprise, and laugh together at how they fooled us. But they kept dancing. Queen spun around and around, and each time I could see her face she was grinning. Until after a moment her face was nothing but a grin. Her skin was gone, her muscle gone and she was bare naked, a skeleton just like Wolf had been, and was again. They danced further and further away, and just as they were nearly out of sight, I saw her one last time raise her hand up and wave to all the people on the land who weren't looking. And then once for me.

And then she and Wolf were gone, and we never did see them again. But out by the bog during the right kind of summer night, if there's a real good party going on, every now and then I hear something like a laugh. See something like shadows dancing cross the water.

Dancing Girls

I'm going to tell you a story. About my youngest brother. You're at that age now where you have to hear these things even if you don't like it. See, what you're feeling ain't all that special. It happens to all of us, at some point or another. What really matters is how you handle it.

Jerome was my youngest brother's name. We called him Stargazer though, 'cause he was always going around just gawking at shit like he was half in some other world. Jerome smoked a lot, but the dude hit the blunt just two times, and he would get out of his mind high. He was always coming up with some of the craziest shit you could only ever half believe. But this story is true. I know 'cause I'm telling it. So listen, alright?

Down the block there were these girls. Twelve of them, and each just as hot to trot as the next. They all lived in the same apartment complex, and during the day, they'd all sit around their stoop, faces made up, long legs stretched out. They were the talk of the neighborhood.

Shit was just starting to warm up and everybody was getting an itch in their jeans. Even I started running around with a dude from down the street, and usually I didn't go in for that sort of thing. I had sense. But it was just that time of year. Everybody was looking to get some. The neighborhood was full up on bodies just floating around from yard to yard. Sprawling in grass, sitting on porches, sipping beer.

And Stargazer? Well, he wasn't exactly unpopular if you catch my drift. He had enough girls hanging around him that he shoulda been happy. Boy was like a bulb, attracting any gnat without a brain that happened to come within a forty-foot radius of him. He had one of the sweetest faces, with these big brown eyes, and a smile that could cut you. On top of that, he was selling whatever he didn't smoke himself. He had his merits, you see, but he just didn't give a fuck for the girls that were hanging around him. Stargazer was all hung up on The Twelve like every other fool in the neighborhood. All drooling and chasing after 'em like they was dogs and the girls had steak under their skirts.

Thing about these girls is they wouldn't have shit to do with none of the dudes. They just sat there sunbathing, talking to each other, rubbing their feet like they'd just run a marathon. They always had the finest clothes and shit, like they were working some Big-Time job, or running around with some Big-Time player. Gleaming like life was one big party. But nobody, and I mean nobody, ever saw them out anywhere. And anytime anyone tried to talk to any of 'em, they just side eyed 'em till they felt so small they had to go away.

When dusk hit—which is when shit really started to get social—they'd stand themselves up, and one by one file back into their building. Then they'd be in all night. Sometimes some young fool would get so fixated on 'em he'd start sneaking into the building and waiting in the hall, listening outside their door. They'd do this a few nights, and then come to their senses and feel ashamed of how dumb they'd been acting or something. 'Cause they wouldn't be around after that. They'd just vanish.

So you see what I'm saying? It was all a great mystery. And that only made the dudes want the Twelve even worse.

My mom hated those girls. When she saw Stargazer getting his head all wrapped around 'em she started to get really worried. Kept going wild on him. "Girls like that," she said, "they ain't nothing but trouble, you hear me? You keep away from 'em."

But Stargazer never heard her. It was one of his talents.

So she asked me to keep an eye on him. Ma was working the night shift as a 9-1-1 dispatcher, and she didn't have time to really keep tabs on us. So I was the one who was supposed to have sense and keep Stargazer in line.

But I was fancying myself in love. So I told her yeah, but I really just wanted her and Stargazer off my back so I could kick it with my own dude. Still, I warned Stargazer to keep his distance, and asked my dude what he knew about The Twelve . He didn't really get where I was coming from, though. All he did was tell me he'd never have anything to do with some cold ass bitches like them, and squeezed me hard all over, smiling.

Being told no and being warned just made my brother more goofy. He kept hanging around their stoop trying to get them to talk. Offered 'em beer, weed, anything their hearts desired. They weren't having any of it. The oldest, she musta been somewhere around twenty, had this long black glossy hair and these plump lips like whoa, she straight up cold-shouldered him hard enough that any other dude woulda gave up. But my brother kept at it.

He had a soft spot for the youngest, and though she didn't talk to him, she didn't exactly look away when he came down the street neither.

He was telling me all about her one night when me and my dude were chilled out on my couch. How she had these eyes soft as black velvet and shit. Waxing poetic like cats only do when they got it real bad.

"You better quit while you're ahead," I told him, "or you're gonna make a straight-up ass out of yourself." I looked to my dude for help and he shifted his arm out from under me and laid back, blowing smoke out his nostrils. He rolled the blunt in his hand, looked my brother in the eye.

"She's right," he said. "It's not a good look for a dude to be chasing after some bitch like this. You got girls lined up enough. Just fuck a few of them and be done with it."

"It ain't like that," Stargazer said.

"Ain't nothing that'll get your mind off it better," my dude said.

"Maybe I don't wanna get my mind off her," Stargazer said. "Maybe this is real. Like, maybe it's love."

I snorted then and shook my head. "What makes you think you got any better of a chance then all them other thirsty ass dudes who came before?"

"I got an in," Stargazer said, and he grinned. He dug his hand in his pocket and pulled something out, held it so me and my dude could see. In his palm there was this tiny little charm, small and silver. A heart. Not a cartoon one but anatomical, and near perfect like it could start beating at any moment. "See?"

"So?" I asked.

"It's hers. She dropped it last night before she went in. They all got 'em. Hanging off little chains round their ankles. But I saw that hers was gone. When they went in I searched around and found it in the grass. I'ma go tonight and give it back to her."

"And this is going to get you what, exactly?" I asked.

Stargazer shrugged and took the blunt from my dude. He hit it and let the smoke seep out of his teeth. "We'll see," he said.

That night I was too busy to keep an eye on my fool brother. It was Friday, and everyone in the neighborhood was making plans. Me and my dude were hitting up house after house, drinking and laughing up a storm. It was exactly what I thought life should be like, you know, when you're in love. Everywhere we went he kept his hands on my hips, and I let my head sit back against his chest. Every joke I told he would reach up and stroke my cheek, laughing. And once, when we were so high off each other, so buzzed and in love, I took off this little jade ring I was wearing and slipped it on his pinky.

"Keep it," I said, "so you always got something of me on you."

And he laughed and unhooked his watch and put it around my wrist. It was so big it wouldn't stay put, so with every step I could feel it there, thumping against my hand.

It was perfect, right then.

So I wasn't too worried about my little brother and his impending heart break. Shit like that is something we all go through at one point or another, and sometimes the best thing to do is just let it happen so a lesson can be learned.

'Sides, I had other plans for the night. Plans that would work best if my brother wasn't at home. Plans that involved privacy. So when I took my dude's hand and led him into my house, and we found it empty, I didn't go looking for him exactly. You know?

<3

Next day Stargazer slipped in right before dawn. His clothes were all rumpled and smelled like smoke. Not just weed but those big ass cigars that old men love. The kind that sit in their mouths thick as dicks and can make you hurl if you aren't careful. Me and my dude had just put ourselves back together, and I was cooking eggs in the kitchen while he watched.

Stargazer sat himself down in a chair across from my dude, this stupid dreamy grin plastered on his face. Just humming till I asked where he'd been. Which is all he'd been waiting for, so he could tell us the whole thing. It went something like this:

Stargazer went up to the youngest with the soft eyes and crouched down next to her so the others couldn't see what he was up to. He showed her the charm she'd lost and she got all flustered and her hand went down to her ankle to see that it was actually gone. Instead of taking it back though she closed Stargazer's fingers 'round it, and whispered for him to come back later that night. Round ten. Apartment 7a. That's what she told my brother, and so that's what he did.

When he got there he knocked on the door, but it wasn't the youngest who opened it. The oldest of The Twelve was standing there, dressed in all black leather, like some kind of cat suit, a belt made of silver chains looped around her hips. She was giving him a look so cold he wanted to run, but instead he pulled the charm out of his pocket and showed it to her. She huffed and called over her shoulder. The youngest came bounding to the door.

My brother said the oldest pulled a thin chain from around her waist and linked it through the charm. Then wrapped the chain around his wrist, leaving enough for the youngest to take in hand like a leash.

"He's your dog, so you watch him," the eldest said, then she went back into the apartment.

The youngest smiled up at him and gave the leash a tug. He felt the silver squeeze his wrist and his arm jerk forward of its own will. She led him back into the apartment with the girls. They were in a bedroom too small for so many of them, and had their clothes out everywhere. The girls were throwing this and that on, lining their lips and powdering each other like they were about to hit the streets hard. The youngest tied my brother's chain to a lamp and joined the rest of them, and for the longest, he just sat there, quiet and watching.

Then when they were all done the eldest rolled back the throw-rug and stomped her foot on the wood floor three times. A panel of it slid back like some kind of James Bond shit to reveal a deep hole. The girls slipped into it one by one. The youngest came and untied my brother and led him after her. Down she jumped, and after her my brother fell.

My brother didn't say so but I know he musta been shrieking. Cat hated heights. But when they hit the ground it was soft as feathers, even though he said they fell for a long ass time. Like the world had open up and swallowed 'em.

The light was low where they landed, but my brother told me he'd fallen on a mattress. Covered in pillows and soft silky blankets. It smelled like rose perfume, and not the cheap burning kind you buy at Family Dollar, but like real roses. Like a garden.

He felt a tug on his chain and he got up to follow it. He was being taken down a flight of stairs. With each step the light grew a little brighter until he could finally make out the silhouettes of the girls walking before him. He could hear music pulsing somewhere below. He could smell smoke.

"Where are we going?" my brother asked, but The Twelve only shushed him.

The flight of stairs opened up to a large, circular room, lit by black lights and small candles burning on low tables. On one side there was a bar, black and polished to shine with tubes running round the length of it, filled with small purple lights. At the back of the room there was a stage that branched out into a small circle in the middle, complete with a golden pole. To one side there was a small tiled section left open for dancing, and a door of heavy iron beyond that with a small sliding window at head height.

The girls split apart laughing and spread themselves out at several tables. The eldest took the stairs up to the stage. The youngest lead Stargazer to their own table, and they sat down together.

"What is this place?" Stargazer asked, but the youngest put a finger against her lips.

"Ssh," she said. "I like this song."

The eldest made her way to the circular island of stage in the center of the room. Laughing, she gripped the pole in her hands and spun around it, her hair a long dark wave rolling out behind her. Then she stamped her heel three times, and the iron door opened. In came two of the biggest, scarred, spookiest mugs my brother said he ever saw. Seven foot tall, maybe bigger, he thought, with bodies like boulders. One carried a stool with him, set it down next to the door and perched there. The other made his way to the bar and started pouring drinks. The eldest slid off the stage and sat at her own table, tossing her hair over her shoulder.

The bartender loaded the drinks up on a platter and made

the rounds, dropping a drink down in front of each girl. Each girl cooed and gave him a pat on his big, mangled cheek. He moved on. When he came to the youngest, he slid a long island in front of her and set a tequila down on the table by my brother.

"Thanks, man," my brother said, giving him a nod. The big man grunted, bared his teeth and went away.

My brother sipped his tequila and the youngest smiled up at him, her pupils big and sparkly as fucking diamonds peeking out from under her lashes. At least that's how my brother told it. They sat there eyeing each other up, my brother trying to think of something to say. Before he could, the music got louder, and the big dude at the door swung it open. In came dude after dude, dressed in fine suits, parcels under their arms. Each one of 'em, my brother said, looked wasted as all hell. Slack jawed like they were on some extra dumb shit.

All the girls but the youngest got up and fluttered over to them, each taking one or two by the arm and leading them to their tables. The extras leftover who just sat wherever or lingered limply around the edges of the room. One tried to sit down at the table with the youngest and my brother, but she flicked her hand up and motioned him away.

The girls flipped their hair and laughed and talked, and the dudes sat there, nodding, mouths agape My brother turned to his girl and opened his mouth but she just put a finger against her lips and smiled.

"I really like this song," she said.

One of The Twelve bounced to her heels and swooped up on stage. A couple of the men gathered at its edge. Like fucking lemmings, my brother said. The girl started to dance. Slow. Grinding on the air like it'd just proposed. The dudes slit the paper packages in their arms open and started pulling all sorts of shit out. Pearls. Fine, shimmering tops and short skirts. Boots. They threw 'em up on stage, one after another, and every now and then the girl stopped to laugh behind her hand. Kick out a foot and hook something with her heel. Push it towards the back where it all started to gather in a pile.

One of 'em pulled out a ring set with a ruby the size of a fucking knuckle, my brother swears. That's when he recognized him; the guy. It was one of the cats that used to hang round The Twelve drooling all the time. Mark, or some shit like that. My brother knew him from around school but hadn't seen him around in forever. Some people thought maybe he got hooked on heroin, or went to jail or something.

Stargazer started to get real nervous. Like maybe something was up. If he'd had any sense he would have left right then and there. But my brother never had any sense. Shit, I don't think most men do, when there's cooch involved.

Right when his feet started to get cold, that's when the youngest pulled the chain round his wrist so his hand was right next to hers. She picked it up off the table and put it against her face.

"Wanna dance?" She asked.

"We danced all night, me and her," Stargazer said, "The girls kept switching partners, and every now and then one of them dudes would come up gawking, but she'd snap her little fingers and he'd bug off. It was just us. It was just me she wanted, y'know? Then at the end of the night, at the door, she pecked me right here." He pressed his thumb against his cheek and smiled really goofy.

"Hm," my dude said. He was rubbing his chin and knitting his brow at my brother hard.

"I'm happy for you," I said, "looks like you got your girl." I didn't say that it sounded a little shady, or if not shady, ridiculous. The whole underground club and that bullshit. I figured Stargazer was high as shit and embellishing. It wouldn't be the first time.

"So you going to see her again?" my dude asked.

"Yeah, I'ma go back tonight," Stargazer said, grinning. My dude shook his head real slow and I laid an egg down on his plate.

"Nah, dude," he kicked his feet out under the table and lifted his fork. Poked the yolk of the egg so it all ran out in yellow rivers along the plate. "You wanna hold up on that. Lemme teach you a few tricks."

My brother followed my dude's advice to a T, which musta been hard since he was pretty much raring to go the whole time. He waited a whole week. Didn't hang around their stoop. Didn't go down to see 'em. Just hung around the neighborhood, super public, laughing loud enough that it could carry down the street and ring in their pretty little ears.

"You make it too easy and she's gonna get bored of your ass. You gotta dangle the bait." That's what my dude said to do and Stargazer did it, even though I said it was a bad plan. And it was killing Stargazer. He kept asking me to walk down there and take a look at her. I did about three or four times. The Twelve caught me staring though, and started to shoot me looks real hard. So I walked on and told my brother if he wanted to see her so bad, he should use his own eyes.

"A dude can't seem too desperate," my dude said. "You gotta

play cool. Let her stew."

"You do this shit to me?" I asked, "Did you let me stew?"

He put his hands on my hips and smiled, said: "Baby, I didn't need to."

I took his hands off of me and cocked my head to the side, looked at him real hard. Like maybe I was looking for the first time.

That Friday my brother dressed himself in his best clothes, bought a new pair of sneakers, and practiced his smile in the mirror all day. The ban was lifted. He could go to her without my dude and the rest of the cats on the block calling him a pussy. Or thirsty. Or whatever the fuck. He flossed and polished and preened until ten. Then he walked out the door and headed to their apartment.

"Remember, act like nothing happened. Like you haven't been gone at all," my dude told him. And then he whispered in my brother's ear, palmed him something. When my brother was gone, I looked him up and down.

"What was that about?" I asked.

"Nothing," he said.

"Don't nothing me."

"I just feel bad for him is all. Dude should have a man around the house. To teach him this shit. I'm just tryin' to help out." He smiled big again and took my hand. Pulled me in close and kissed me on the mouth.

Next day my brother came back. Stinking of booze, and smoke, and sex. Grinning like he was fucking king of more than just a gram of weed, and his own shit-stained shorts. My dude and him clasped hands and knocked their chests together.

My dude said: "You do it?"

And my brother, sweet little Stargazer, he cocked his head back and said: "You know it."

They both laughed, my dude slapped him on the back, and they laughed harder.

"What are you two going on about?" I asked, eyes narrowed like hell 'cause I was pretty sure I knew.

"Last night," my brother said, and he grinned and ducked his head, "Let me just tell you."

So he sits down, and my dude sits down, and I sit down and cross my arms over my chest and get ready to listen.

He went to the apartment and the youngest answered this time. Her eyes were all hopeful but anxious, the way a stray cat's get when you try and offer 'em food. She took a step toward him before hesitating, looking over her shoulder like she's waiting for direction. Then she leaned up against the doorframe and looked him over, cooling.

"Where've you been?" she asked.

"Around," my brother said. Like he was told to, no doubt.

She bit her lower lip, and turned her head away slightly. Stargazer reached out and put a hand on her shoulder.

"What's up, baby," he said. "Can I come in or nah?"

She looked up at him from under her eyelashes and he smiled. She relented. The chain was put back on. He waited while they got ready. Then they went down the hole, and all was as it was the Friday night before. Except this time, 'bout half-way through, Stargazer got up and started talking to the other girls. Before, on the street, they'd cold shoulder him, but down in the underground, they were friendly enough. He made a few jokes about the other dudes—how dull they looked, how stupid—shit like that. They'd laugh behind their hands. He said even the eldest was watching him. Once, when she was hanging off the golden pole, she dipped her body backwards, her hair tumbling down like a waterfall, and held his eyes for a solid minute. He swore.

Well, little girl, the youngest, she was following behind him the whole time, holding on to that chain. But no matter how she tugged it, he kept his attention on other girls. Just like my dude said to, he said. And sure enough, when she looked like she might be ready to cry, my brother turned round and planted his hand round her waist, right up close to her ass.

He kept doing shit like that all night. Ebb and flow. Attend, ignore. After a few drinks and a night full of that she was about out of her mind, I imagine. Ready to do something drastic. Anything.

"And then you fucked her?" my dude asked.

My brother nodded. "She took me up to that mattress where we landed. Got really friendly."

My dude grinned. "I told you, dude. Told you I could get you laid."

My brother squirmed back in his chair, face ate up by his shit eating smile. "Yeah. Shit was legit. Just like you said."

I kept quiet, my tongue pressed tight against my teeth.

So that's how it happened. My brother became a man. Capital M, capital A, capital N. Like that. By mind-fucking a young girl till she fucked him on a mattress a few stair flights away from a club.

He went from sweet, if stupid, gawking boy, to full-fledge fucking Man. And don't think he didn't act like it made the sun shine out his very own ass. He bagged one of The Twelve. What's worse? He said after he was pretty sure she was a virgin. Damn.

He tried to tell every motherfucker in the neighborhood. Only he couldn't. Every time he opened his mouth to say it, it was like the words gunked up in his throat. Or suddenly someone was talking much louder than him, and nobody was paying attention. Small mercy that. It didn't seem to work under our own roof. He went on about it. And my dude listened, rapt as all hell every time. Got to the point where I was about to lose my mind if I heard it once more.

"You don't go around running your mouth about the shit we do, right?" I asked my dude after about the seventh or eighth time.

"Course not, baby," he said and smiled big. But after that I couldn't walk down the street without feeling like the cats on their porches were giving me the eye. Watching me like they knew, or some shit. I was hearing faint hoots and whoops everywhere I went, but when I turned around shit was quiet and still as a desert. I was getting sick of it. Of everything. I was supposed to have sense.

My brother developed a routine. He'd wait a week. He'd go. He'd play his games. He'd fuck the girl. He wasn't dopey eyed about it anymore. Now she was a laugh. A puzzle that he knew all the pieces to. Gone were the days of eyes like velvet. Now it was all coarse shit. Shit that made you want to take a bath after. Each time my dude and him would laugh, and each time I felt a little further from them both. Like I was untethering. I'd float off until they'd talk about something else, and I'd feel safe enough to come back. But each time I got a little less close than I had before.

My brother may have been a lot of things before, but I never expected him to become a jackass. But he was a man now. A player. He started popping his collar, wearing his hats real high and walking with a certain swagger I couldn't stand.

He started talking about the eldest. Not the way he talked about the youngest, mind, but just as much. Her tits. How she had started looking at him more and more often. How sometimes when he looked back, she didn't stop. Her ass.

"You gonna tap that?" my dude asked.

"Shit, I don't know," my brother said.

My dude popped his feet up on our coffee table. "If you don't, I will," he laughed.

I heard it but I didn't bother saying anything. Just set my beer down and went up to my room. Alone.

Not long after that my brother didn't come back home. He was gone a day. Then a night. Then another day. By the third our mother had noticed what was up and had started wigging out on me something fierce. Asking where he was, where he'd been, had I seen him. I tried to tell her to chill out. That her little sweet baby boy was a man now. It wasn't exactly stars he was gazing at anymore. But she wouldn't hear it. She told me I had to go out and find him.

"And if you don't come home with him," she said, "don't come home at all."

That suited me just fine, I wanted to tell her. I was getting sick of everyone in the neighborhood. Sick of my own dude, who wasn't even really my dude anymore. How could he be when he said the shit he did? When he hardly came around? How could he have ever been? I left his watch in the bottom of my dresser and tried to forget about him. I was that sick of shit.

Hell, I was even sick of my own family. Couldn't even trust my baby brother to be decent. So who was there to trust at all?

But I still went to look for him, since I had a pretty good idea where to start.

The Twelve were out on their porch as usual, looking more fine and more happy than I'd ever seen them before. Their lips were plumper. Their eyes brighter. Their hair glowing. Or maybe I'd just never gotten that close to them before. Or looked as hard. The only one who looked sorta rough was the youngest, but she looked rough the way most girls do. On the inside, with only a little bit of it showing through. Near the eyes. It was something most people wouldn't notice. Something you had to know to look for. Like maybe you felt that way yourself, one time or another. Other than that she was just as perfect as the rest.

I stepped straight up to the eldest and I asked her, real firm: "Where's my brother?"

"Why you asking me?" she said. "When you oughta check with your dude. I have a feeling they're together."

All the girls smiled really slyly to one another, and touched their lips like there was a laugh waiting behind 'em. I put my hands on my hips and thrust my jaw out, ready to let them know I wasn't fucking around.

"You can feed me shit all you like but it doesn't mean I'm gonna swallow it. I know my brother was here, and I know you have something to do with him being gone."

The eldest just rolled her eyes, flicked her hair over her shoulder and leaned back. "Girl, you better settle down. Why do you care so much anyhow? We haven't done a thing to you. And your brother? Shit, you ever consider the world's better off with him being gone?"

"Just 'cause someone's an asshole doesn't mean they deserve to just disappear," I said.

The eldest smiled real big. She stretched out her back and ran her hands through her hair. It fanned out behind her on the steps. Her hands swung back around and she cupped them in front of her. "You sure about that?" She asked.

In her palms, just sitting there, was the little jade ring. The one I had slipped off my finger and onto my dude's. The one he'd been wearing ever since. I looked up at the eldest and our eyes touched. And I saw it. The same look the youngest had but older. More buried and a little more like venom. Then I saw it in all of them.

The sun was just about to set, and shit was just about to get social. I heard the woofs, the hollers, the catcalls I'd been hearing for the past few weeks blooming behind me. I turned my face towards them, but a hand on my cheek pulled my eyes back to The Twelve . The youngest was up on her feet, holding me steady.

"Forget about them," she said. "And come inside."

"You ain't exactly the first to feel this way," the eldest told me. And looking at her, I could see it was true. Under the lowlights of the club, in the dark of the underground, things were more obvious. At least to me. Things were more true and less pretty.

"What happened?" I asked her. "To them?" I nodded my head

towards the dudes as they came in. One after the other. All slack jawed like my brother had mentioned, but not in a way I've ever seen a drug do to a person. There was hardly a shadow of who they were left, other than their skins. This was something beyond just dazed. Something my brother should have seen from the start.

"Feels like you're being ate up from the inside, don't it? Feels like there's something wrong inside of you. Like you've been poisoned. Like your body ain't even yours," she said. One of the big, hulking dudes laid a drink down on the table and a hot plate. On it there were hunks of meat. Red and marbled, cut into small squares with small toothpicks stuck in 'em. The eldest picked one up and popped it between her plump lips. She dabbed her mouth where its juice had started to ooze out.

The big husky dude, he brought me over my own drink. The eldest slid the plate over to me. "Try some," she said. "It goes down easy." I picked up one of the little toothpicks and looked it over. It looked tender and fatty. Pulsed almost like jello along with the throbbing music. I took it between my teeth and chewed. It was cold, but alright.

"You want to dance?" She asked me, palm out.

And I did.

My brother brings gold to the youngest. Gifts overflow from his cupped palms. Silk. Fine things. Soft things. They sit at a table together, and he doesn't say shit. They dance together without touching. Round her ankle, the little heart charm thumps in time with the movement of her feet. My dude is there, too. By the stage, drooling and smiling big.

You aren't the first to feel this way, that's all I'm trying to say.

But you have a choice. In how you wanna handle that feeling.

In the underground there's always a steady beat. You can hear it even when the music isn't on. It'll get to be something like your favorite song. Get to where it's like it's in your bones. Do you hear it?

Do you wanna dance?

Curlew

There was a woman that died and left behind something important. Her youngest daughter was sent to bring it to her. To keep it safe it was placed inside of a curlew.

The daughter was picked because she looked the most like her mother. They both had the same patch of discolored skin on their wrist that looked white as an eggshell. The bird was fat with a long curved black beak, and it sat in the crook of her arm as she walked. When it got hungry it leaned its neck forward and nipped the discolored skin on her wrist.

"Feed me," the curlew said.

"Tell me what my mother left behind," the girl replied. But the curlew wouldn't. Instead it offered her a song. She sat down with it in her lap on the side of the road and let it eat seeds from her palm. When it was finished, she took off her shoes and rubbed her feet while the bird sang. All it could manage were two long, stuttering notes that it repeated over and over again. As if someone kept interrupting a tea kettle.

Nearby a lily shook its blossom at them. "There's nothing beautiful about that," it said. "If you're going to see your mother, you should bring her something beautiful."

"You're right," said the girl. She plucked the lily from the ground and fed it to the curlew. After she laid down with the curlew tucked under her head, and she fell asleep. Beneath her ear, she could hear the bird's light and rapid heartbeat. As if someone were flipping through the pages of a book, over and over. When she dreamed, she dreamed of her mother sitting on their stoop, darning socks. Her face was a stone slab; grave, unreadable. She pricked her finger on the needle and blood unfurled from the tip in one long ribbon that kept unraveling. Her mother wove it into the sock. The girl wanted to feel something, but she didn't.

She woke up to the curlew nipping her wrist. She put her shoes back on, placed the curlew back in the crux of her arm, and walked.

They walked far enough that the seams of her shoes began to split, letting little rocks and pebbles slip in and prick her heels. Every few steps she shook them out and they would gleefully roll away covered in a light sheen of her blood. She spat at them and complained each time.

"You'll grow calluses, and it'll hurt less," the curlew said.

"I used to have beautiful feet," she said.

"There were lots of things that used to be this or that and aren't now, and many of those things are better off not being what they were, or even being nothing at all."

"Screw you," she said, and the two lapsed into a sullen silence that was only broken much later by the sound of a hubbubing brook. The curlew reached its long beak forward and bit the girl's discolored wrist so she would stop.

"I'm thirsty," it said. "Take me to the river so I can drink."

"Tell me what my mother left behind." But the curlew wouldn't. Instead, it offered her a feather.

So the girl sat down by the stream and held the bird so it could dip its curved beak into the water. When it was full it plucked a feather out of its back and gave it to the girl. The moment it touched her palm, a wind blew and carried the feather to the stream. It touched down on the surface of the water, and floated out of sight before the girl could even blink.

"Give me another," the girl said.

"One was the deal," said the curlew.

The girl was about to take the curlew and dump it in the river, when the small bubbles escaping from a pebble in the riverbed caught her eye. She leaned towards them, and as each popped she heard whispering.

"That feather was so fragile. So temporary. If you're going to your mother you should bring her something solid and of substance."

"You're right," said the girl. She reached her arm in and plucked the stone from the riverbed then fed it to the curlew.

Then she settled back against a tree and dipped her bare feet into the river. She placed the curlew in her lap. "When I die, I won't leave anything behind," she said.

"Nothing?" The curlew asked.

"Not a name, nor a memory, not even a scrap of hair. That's how death is supposed to be."

"If you say so," said the curlew.

Then the girl closed her eyes. Against her stomach she could feel the warmth of the curlew, and the churn of the water in its stomach as it breathed in and out. She drifted off to sleep, and in her dreams she was being carried by the ribbon down a flight of stairs that circled deeper and deeper into the earth with no visible end. The walls were red velvet, and lined with portraits of her mother's face. The face she had when she had been ill. She looked away from them towards her own body and saw the ribbon splitting her wrist where her birthmark had been.

She woke to someone touching her face.

He was a simple kind of man. There was nothing great nor nothing horrible about him. He had a horse, and some bread, and he offered her a ride as far as he was going. She rode behind him with the curlew tucked between her legs, and her arms wrapped around his chest. When they got to his house he dismounted and looked up at her.

"You look like you could use a hot meal," he said.

The curlew reached its beak up and nipped her wrist but she brushed it off and took the bird up in her arms. Then she dismounted and followed the man inside. He fed her, he drew her a bath, and all the while she carried the bird either in her arms or on her lap. All the while it nipped at her and she brushed its beak away. Then, when night had set in, she followed him into his bed, and set the curlew on the floor.

After a few days, he offered to make a cage.

The curlew's cage was hung from a brass pole in his room, next to the window. During the night she kept a sheet draped over it, but when the moon was out the light would seep through and she could see its silhouette through the thin fabric. Then she dreamed of ribbons, her mother's lined face, a thin-lipped scowl, calloused feet, pricked fingers on wrinkled hands. In the morning she took the sheet down, and the curlew reached its beak through the bars to nip her wrist.

"Open the cage," it said.

"Tell me what my mother left behind," she replied. Each time it refused, and offered her something else. An egg. Its eye. Its tongue. Each time she walked away without accepting.

Autumn came, and she grew fatter. Her hands and feet grew swollen. The man came home later and later into the night, and she would sit on the bed, folding clothes and watching the silhouette of the curlew. She started feeding it less and less, and yet it remained as plump and round as the day she started carrying it. In fact, it looked even bigger.

Night crept towards early morning. She ran out of clothes to fold and put away. She went to the curlew's cage and took the sheet down to shake the dust out of the creases and the bird opened one eye to watch her. She ran the sheet through her hands and waited for the curlew to ask for its freedom.

"Do you want to know what your mother left behind?" it asked. She let the sheet slip through her hands, and turned to the bird. It eased its beaks through the bars of the cage and she knelt to put her ear near it.

"Sorrow," the curlew said. "And it will be yours until you bring it back to her."

"You're a liar," the girl said.

"My dear, do you know that you're pregnant?"

She picked the sheet back off the floor and draped it over the curlew's cage.

<3

She woke when the man crawled into the bed with her. The sun was up, but he had taken the sheet from the curlew's cage and draped it over the window, so that the light in the room was still dim. She reached out and touched a hand to his chest.

"I have a headache," he said, rolling away.

"I'm pregnant," she said back. She moved towards him and pressed the lump of her belly against his back. He sat up and looked down at her.

"You can't be pregnant," he said. "You have to be married to be pregnant."

"Isn't this a sort of marriage?" She asked.

"You're just a girl I found on the road," he said. "How do I know it's not some other man's you married and bedded before?"

"You know because you know," she said, sitting up. She tried to take his hand and press it to her stomach, but he pushed her away and got out of the bed.

"I don't know. I don't know you, I don't know why you have that bird, and I don't know who put that filthy seed in your belly. But I know I want you gone by tomorrow." He left the room, and before she could untangle herself from the sheets, he was gone again out the front door. She pulled herself to her feet, and went to the window in time to see him riding off on the horse that had carried her there.

The curlew watched her watch him go.

"I used to move so easily, but now my body is a stranger to me." She went to the cage and placed her hand on the door. "I don't want my mother's sorrow."

"If you open the cage, I can fix it," the curlew said.

She lifted the bar locking the curlew in, and opened the door.

CURLEW

The curlew came into her arms.

"Lay down on the bed, and close your eyes" the curlew said. The girl did as she was told, with the curlew on her breast. It stood and made its way over the growing mound of her stomach. It dipped its long beak into her navel. It burrowed beneath her skin, then further.

She fed the fetus to the curlew.

The curlew came back into her arms, and laid its head on her collarbone. Together, they slept, and she dreamed her mother was a giant. She dreamed the blood trickling from her navel was the red ribbon leading up her mother's legs, curving around her thighs, pouring from a wound hidden under her mother's dress. She was climbing it. Above her the curlew landed, its beak sharpened thin as scissors. It took the ribbon in its mouth.

Its beak closed and she fell.

She woke at dusk and the curlew was waiting by the bedroom door. Her navel was twisted closed in a tight black scab, encircled by dried blood. The swelling of her stomach had gone down. She put on the clothes she had come in. She picked the curlew up off the floor and tucked it under her arm. She left, and made her way back into the forest.

She kept walking. The curlew never nipped her wrist to ask for food, or for water, or for rest. It never slept, but kept its head angled up so that its long beak would rest against her breast. She walked for days, until her shoes came apart completely. The rocks came, and pricked her feet, and rolled away, but she took no notice.

Soon the trees shed their leaves, and all around her they looked like torched skeletons lifting their splintered bones towards the sky. Then snow fell and coated their limbs, and the whole world looked like a silhouette beneath a great hung sheet. Snow coated her hair, her shoulders, and the curlew, and still she kept walking.

She came to a place where the snow gave way to a patch of hard stone that stretched a mile long and wide. When she came to the center, she found a red door sunk into the rock. She clutched the curlew to her breast and bent over to open it.

Behind it were the stairs.

There was only darkness once the door swung closed behind her. She had to feel the edge of each step with her foot, and brace her hand against the wall. It felt warm and soft, as if she were brushing up against a living animal. Every now and then she would misstep and the curlew would rustle in the crook of her arm.

"Why are you so afraid? You can fly, can't you?" She said.

"I don't think I can anymore."

She shifted it in her arm and realized how heavy it had become. Like a stone. She reached her hand up to touch its body. Beneath its feathers, it felt hard and bloated. She closed her eyes and it made no difference, the dark was so complete. She pressed forward, her hand massaging the curlew's back.

After a long time, there were no more stairs, and she was walking along a long corridor towards a dim light. When she reached it, the hallway opened up to a cavern of stone that stretched so far above her she couldn't see the ceiling. There were small cottages, and tracks worn in the rock by the passing of feet. People were there, some who had the same patch of egg-white skin on their necks, their faces, their breasts and arms, as her and her mother.

She had come to the hall of her ancestors.

She looked to the curlew, whose eyes were half-lidded, and whose beak hung open. She put the bird to her ear and could hear something whistling inside.

She went to a woman and asked after her mother. She pointed her onward. After some time, she asked a man, and he too pointed her on. She kept asking, and each person looked at her with the same set of eyes, the same worn face, that her mother had worn all her life. Any could have been her, but they kept waving her on.

Eventually one pointed to a young woman nearby, laying on the stone floor with her hands folded under her head. The woman was whistling tunelessly. The girl asked the woman her name, and she received her mother's in reply. But this woman was young, and smooth skinned, and smiling like an idiot up at nothing.

"I'm your daughter," the girl said. The woman tilted her head back and looked at the girl and blinked. The girl held the curlew out. Its breath was faint and whistling. She could see patches of skin through its feathers. "This is for you."

The woman blinked again. "A daughter? There's some mistake. I don't have a daughter. And I don't want your bird. It looks sick."

"The bird is mine. It's the thing inside that's yours."

"What's that?"

"Something important."

"What is it?" The woman sat up and unfolded her arms, and on her wrist the girl saw the same patch of milky white skin.

"It's yours."

"But what?" The woman narrowed her eyes. In between the girl's fingers, the bird gave one shuddering breath, and then began heaving. Out of its beak poured tar. It splattered on the cave floor and congealed into a ball. The curlew went limp. The girl put the bird to her ear and heard nothing. She put her mouth around its beak and blew breath into it, pumped its chest, but the bird stayed limp. She bit her tongue and held the bird to her chest.

The woman took one look at the ball of tar at the girl's feet, then the girl and her dead bird.

"I don't want that," she said. She got to her feet and walked away

The girl tucked the curlew under her shirt so that it laid against her breast, and then she picked up the ball of tar and followed after the woman. The woman ran, so the girl ran. The woman's body was light, and she bounced easily from foot to foot, but the floor was hard, and sharp, and the girl's feet were more suited to the stone. Soon the woman stopped running and started to limp. The girl grabbed her by her hair and pulled her head back.

"Take it," she said, shoving the tar towards the woman's face. The woman turned away from it and shook her head. She spoke through clamped teeth.

"A good daughter would carry her mother's sorrow for her."

"A good mother would never ask her daughter to do that."

The woman writhed and the girl reinforced her grip on her. They fell to the floor together, the ball of tar wedged between them.

"Just take it," the girl hissed. "It's yours to keep. Yours, and it has nothing to do with me."

"How do I know you're my daughter anyway? I don't remember having any children. You think you can show up here and just shove your bird's puke down my throat?"

The girl reached back and curled her fist. She punched her

mother in the jaw. For a moment the woman stilled and the girl climbed on top of her.

"This is what you gave me," she said, pointing to her birthmark. "And this is why they gave me your sorrow. But I don't want it. I have enough of my own."

The woman opened her mouth to protest and the girl took the ball of tar and shoved it deep down the woman's throat. She pulled her hand out and held the woman's mouth closed as she thrashed. Eventually she stilled, gave in and swallowed. Beneath the girl she aged into the mother she had known.

The girl stood up and took the curlew out of her shirt. She held its limp body in her hands, cupping its head in one palm. On the floor her mother wept and clawed the rock as if trying to bury herself all over.

She knelt down, cradling the bird in one arm, and touched her mother's face. "I'm sorry," she said. "I had to."

"Stay with me," her mother asked. "Don't leave me alone with this."

The girl shook her head, and her mother clutched onto her. "Here," the girl said. She placed the nail of her finger to the curlew's chest. She split it down the middle and pried it apart with her hands. She tipped the curlew over, and out poured pebbles. They scattered on the stone floor and rolled together into a small, roofless cottage.

Then came the lilies. They grew out of the slit and up along the cottage. They curled inward and circled along the stone to make a carpet of vines and flowers. Then a bed, a table, a chair. They continued growing and blossoming, until it was fully furnished with flowers of every color. Then they grew outward into a small roof, and their roots twisted out of the curlew and embedded themselves into the stone.

From out of the curlew's belly the girl pulled a babe, small and smooth, with a perfect patch of egg white skin on her wrist. She passed the babe to her mother.

"Take these," she said. "They'll make it lighter."

Her mother took the babe and looked to her daughter. "But what will you keep?" She asked.

The girl tucked the curlew in her mouth and closed it. She stood up and gave her mother, the cottage, and the babe one last look. She turned and she swallowed.

I'll Tell You a Love Story

You'll have to forgive me for waiting to tell this to you when you're sleeping, but it's the only way I can do it. If you could see yourself stretched out on the floor, laying in the pool of light from the streetlamp right outside our window—how it very nearly looks like moonlight, and how very nearly beautiful you are—you'd understand why. Or maybe you wouldn't. But I'm going to go ahead and do it anyway.

This story is about a pair of lovers, which makes it not so different from our own. Only they didn't meet outside of a bar while one smoked a cigarette, and the other tried to fix her broken pump. They also weren't in their late twenties, a little bit angry and a little bit bored, trapped in a shitty city while the world's economy tanked. They lived in the once upon a time days, on a small island, the kind with palm trees and small little monkeys that would look good in bell boy caps. It was like paradise, probably. And they met when they were very young. Just kids, even. The way people who are in love are supposed to.

He was a kind man with a broad chest, and just the right length of hair and the right amount of stubble. He had a mole over one of his eyebrows, but not the gross kind. It was the kind people find endearing. When I picture him, I see Cary Grant. You don't have to, though. I know how much you hate him. To be honest, you'd probably hate this guy, too. He didn't cuss excessively, or spit, or fight, or drink too much like other men. Maybe he didn't talk a lot, but his silence was never out of coldness, or because he was dull. He wanted to make sure he only ever said the right things, is all. He wasn't the kind of dude that caused anyone harm just for harm's sake, or out of ignorance, or anything like that.

The woman was tall and slender, with skin as white and soft as three-ply ultra plush toilet paper. She had long black hair that she always kept neat, and eyes the shape and color of almonds. And her lips? I could spend hours telling you about how soft they were and how sweet they tasted, but I only have so long, and it would probably just get upsetting. Besides, he didn't love her for her lips, or because she was beautiful. There are plenty of beautiful women everywhere. Just being beautiful is boring and overrated. He loved her because she was her. She was honest, loyal, and gentle. She'd never even killed a bug. Not even once, I swear. And she was clever, too, with a musical little laugh. Delicate, I guess is the word I'm looking for. Not at all like a donkey braying, or a grandma wheezing, or that kind of thing.

So anyway, he loved her, and she loved him, and their life was wonderful. Every morning he went out on the ocean, and caught fish. She tended to the house and worked in the garden, growing their vegetables, fruits, and other stuff. At night they added the spoils of their labor together into a lovely dinner. They swapped stories about their days, read each other poetry, told each other jokes—they never ran out of things to say. Even if it did get quiet, it was never tense. It'd just be because they were too busy loving each other to speak. After, they laid together in the light of the actual moon, and he stroked her hair, and she kissed his chin, and it was utterly, devastatingly perfect. That really is the only word for it. Perfect.

Then one day he came across a group of not-so-perfect kids beating up on this turtle with sticks, pelting it with stones, spitting on it, and in general just being snot-nosed little jerks. Being the kind, considerate, perfect dude he was, he chased them off. The turtle was looking pretty worse for wear, so the man tended to his wounds as best as he could, and helped him get back to the water.

The turtle was so grateful he invited the man to come and see his kingdom at the bottom of the ocean. The turtle was a king, by the way. A real fancy hotshot one. And when a talking turtle king invites you to the bottom of the ocean to see his castle, you go, right? Besides, he figured it would make a good story to tell his wife when he got home. He figured he'd only be gone a few hours, and they didn't try to own each other, like some couples do. They didn't need to know where the other one was at all times, or who they were with, and so on. They let each other live their lives, you know? So he figured there was no harm in it.

He rode on the turtle's back out into the ocean and down to the very, very bottom where the sun can't even reach. They have to use those glowing plankton to see down there. All around their turtle city and in their turtle homes they have them strung up like Christmas lights. The turtle gave the man a tour of his castle. He showed him his throne, his concubines, all his fancy jewels, everything. He even introduced him to the Ocean, as in the Goddess. They ate a wonderful meal of oysters, seaweed, and other ocean-floor foods, like maybe eel, and they drank wine, danced, and joked around. The whole time the man was thinking about his wife—about how she'd never believe him. How great it would be to tell her everything. And above all else, he was thinking about how much he loved her. After just a few hours, he started missing her.

He told the turtle he wanted to go home, but the turtle said he couldn't. He said that the Ocean had taken a liking to him, and he had to stay. The man insisted that the turtle had to take him back to the surface. The turtle insisted he could do no such thing. He wasn't allowed to. The turtle may be a king, but the Ocean was a Goddess, and typically, Goddesses tend to get their way.

The man said he would swim back, and the turtle warned him it would take a very long time. In fact, the turtle said, he had already been gone a very long time. A much longer time than he thought. Time moves different deep down in the ocean. Years and years and years had passed, the turtle said, so the man may as well stay.

Instead the man took off in a panic, swimming as fast as he could despite the turtle's calls for him to come back, and the Ocean's changing the current to try and pull him down. He fought it, thinking only of his wife, and how sad she must have been waiting all alone for years, not even knowing where he was. He wasn't worried at all that she may have moved on. He knew she would wait, because that's how strong their love was. They weren't the kind of people who'd give up on each other.

She was waiting. He knew that for a fact.

And he was right. When he hadn't come back that first day, his wife had gone down to the beach to look for him. She stayed there all day and all night, burning in the hot sun till her toilet paper skin dried and cracked; and shivering when the moon rose and the wind came howling across the water. She stayed the next day, too. And the next day. Writing his name in the sand so that the waves would come, swallow it, and hopefully carry it to him wherever he may be. She kept writing, and she kept waiting, until she grew old and weak. Even then she stayed, and lived on just hoping she might see him again.

For 100 years he swam, and for 100 years she was on the beach, waiting. And she was still there when he finally climbed to shore. But by then she had died, and it was only her bleached skeleton that was there to greet him. Still, he knew it was her. He would recognize her even if she were nothing more than a cluster of dust motes he accidentally breathed in.

So he went to her, still dripping from head to toe with water, and pruney as a sea sponge. He clasped her bones to his broad chest, and he placed his mouth against her teeth, and he kissed her. He kissed her so hard, the waves stilled mid-crest, the Earth slowed its roll, and the little monkeys fell out of the perfect palm trees. It was the kind of kiss that could rewrite the universe. And it did. When his lips touched her teeth, a little of the Ocean's water slipped into her jaw, and worked its way through her, bringing her back to life. Not only that but it made her just as young and beautiful as she ever was.

They wept, kissed each other in every possible place, and did all that other sweet reunion stuff, kneeling right there in the shallow tide. But it didn't last long. The Ocean, jealous and crazy and wanting him, reached out with one huge wave and snatched him up. Though the woman tried to hold on, the Ocean was much stronger than her, and tore him right out of her arms. The Ocean dragged the man back down to the depths. On the beach, the woman waited once more, writing his name again and again. Until the man could get loose and swim back to shore.

There he finds her bones. He kisses her back to life. They shower one another with love for the few seconds they can, and the Ocean catches him up, and drags him back down. And then they do it all over. And all over. One hundred years of swimming, and waiting, and dying. All for that one kiss. All for those few seconds.

See, they aren't the type of people who just walk away. They have passion. They have something real. They wouldn't sleep back to back every night. They wouldn't just stare at the TV whenever the silence gets so unbearable that even the sounds of gunshots and shattering windows are considered welcome reliefs. They're still at it right now. Still swimming, still waiting, still dying, still loving, still working. Because love takes work, right? That's what you're always saying. Love takes work. You just have to want to do it.

And I don't want to.

Please, don't hate me for this. In the morning, try to understand not all kindness looks and feels the same. I may not be willing to swim for you, to wait for you, to die for you, but I am willing to leave for you. And that's probably the kindest thing I could ever do.

Don't you think?

Outbound

Mary turns right into the Religious Department at 9:13 a.m. She knows this because the first thing her eyes do is seek out the large clock hung high on the beige wall. She levels her eyes with the name plates that sit on top of the cubicles. Tombstones, Mary calls them. She sees her own a row back. *Mary St. Peters*.

Her father chose the name because he thought it was funny. Mary for the mother of Christ. St. Peters for the first pope. He loves to laugh, Satan. And he's had many daughters. He's only ever had daughters. And she, the youngest of all of them, is the thirty-sixth Mary. He never gets tired of his jokes. All the other Mary's are long dead by now, and none of them ended up particularly well. But she`s the worst of the lot.

She works at a call center.

She drops down into her chair, checking the cubicles on either side of her. On the right there's a middle-aged man massaging his temples and glowering at the screen. She's seen him often and spoken to him never, which makes him one of her personal favorites. To her left, there's a short, round woman with an upturned nose and a perma-red face. Mary calls her pig-woman. Mary went through training with her. Pig-woman reads with the same flourish and depth of emotion as an ATM.

When the pig-woman sees Mary she pulls the headset mic away from her mouth. "You're late," she says.

Mary nods, and shoves her own headset down over her ears, and logs into the computer without looking towards the woman's red face again. She takes the rosary beads she has looped around her wrist between her thumb and forefinger and massages them slowly. Satan thinks she wears them to be funny, but she needs something during the day to occupy her hands and keep her calm. Besides, when she's wearing them her horns seem to come in slower. This morning, she had woken up to find them nearly grown in completely. It had taken an extra twenty minutes to shave them down. Already she feels them pressing up through her hair and rubbing against the band of her headset.

A blue window pops up on Mary's screen, flickers, turns black, and text appears in the corner. *Jzbl-3690*. Mary sucks her breath between her teeth and slumps back in her chair. Jezebel is one of those hot-shot gospel preachers old Southern Baptists watch every Saturday and Sunday on the church network. She wears ten-thousand-dollar pant suits paid for by donations, and has teeth as white as a virgin's panties. She lives in California, speaks with a Southern accent, and is so full of shit she should have her own line of port-a-potties.

She's also Mary's older, and only full-blooded sister.

Mary hears a rustle to her left followed by a series of crunches. She turns her head slightly, and sees pig-woman sitting splay legged with a bag of potato chips laying open against her crotch. Pig-woman wipes her greasy hands down her stocking and smiles at Mary.

"TGIF," she says through a spray of crumbs. One lands on Mary's skirt.

Mary's headset beeps. She turns to find the script already loaded. Next to her, the man groans, low and throaty.

"Fuck me," he says.

Mary's head aches.

Within the first hour, Mary is already thinking about going home. By ten o'clock she's been hung up on six times, cussed out seven times, and received only one donation of ten dollars from a man who insisted Jezebel use it to build an incinerator for people he referred to as "the gays and all them other perverts."

"They need to be punished," the man insisted, before hanging up.

Mary didn't care much what people did with one another. She had never been into punishing or judging. When she had gone to college, her father had hopes she'd focus on criminal justice. But, as is her custom, she disappointed him and enrolled in the philosophy program instead.

She still has only one donation by eleven. But the hang ups and the cuss outs have skyrocketed. More than usual, she thinks. She gazes often out the small, slim windows along the furthest wall of the office. It gives her a limited view of the smoking pavilion and the parking lot. Soon, she promises herself. Her horns are pushing the band of her headphones off. At the start of each call she has to clamp the headphones to her ear and readjust the mic. Each call gives the headache a tiny nudge towards a migraine. By this point the throbbing in her head is hard enough that she can feel her ears squeezing shut with each pulse. On top of that, her skin`s started to itch. Like she spent the night on an ant pile.

An old man laughs at Mary when she asks him for a fifty-dollar donation. He tells her she can suck his cock. He tells her she sounds just like a whore he knew down in Mexico. He starts going into detail when Mary disconnects the call. Someone could be listening. She knows this is always possible. Her managers will say she did the right thing. But Jezebel would be pissed. And she's for sure listening. She's in town, after all. Last night she'd had dinner with Satan and Mary. She had taken them out to Olive Garden, and picked at a salad while dropping vague hints about the future.

"You're going to be really pleased, I think," she told Satan. "We've been racking up the numbers."

Satan had scowled as he finished sucking up a string of spaghetti and shook his head. "Numbers," he said. "Profits. Margins. I don't understand half the things you say, you know. Back in my day, the only things that mattered were the results you could see. Taste. Feel. The blood on your hands. The wails of the damned. The rage of the Almighty." His eyes darted up towards the ceiling and stayed there for a moment, the lights playing against his cataracts. Mary thought for a moment that he looked younger than she'd seen him in years, then looked at her plate instead.

"Mary killed a cat the other week," Satan said, and she heard his fork scrape against his plate as he began eating again. "Didn't you, Mary?"

Mary nodded and pushed the remains of her dinner into one heap at the side of her plate. Truth was she hit the cat during a rainstorm. It had darted out into the road and straight under the wheel of her car. She had gotten out and scooped its broken body into the car with her, and first began driving to the vet with it bleeding in her lap. Then it gave one last little shudder and its body deflated, so Mary ended up driving to the woods to bury it with a trowel she bought from the dollar store. When she came back covered in rain, blood, and mud, Satan was so excited she couldn't get any of the details out other than there was a cat, and now it was dead, and it was her fault.

"Is that right?" Jezebel looked at Mary, folding her hands on the table and leaning forward. "Well, she's a valuable part of the operation for sure. We wouldn't be able to pull it off without all the little soldiers on the front lines."

"Front lines," Satan said, leaning back and patting his growing beer belly. "I remember those days. Back then, I used to wield a sword that was as long as your whole body, Jezebel. Even in them spikey shoes you wear. And it would burn bright as, well, bright as the fires of hell."

Jezebel nodded. "You've said," she told Satan. But she was still looking at Mary.

"Wasn't no standing there spitting nonsense on the TV, is all I'm saying," Satan said.

Mary wished Satan would stop pussyfooting around and just name Jezebel the new ruler of Hell already. Instead, he's spent the years since his retirement waffling about, pretending Mary was a serious candidate to consider. It was clear to everyone else involved she didn't give a shit about evil. But Satan loved his games, and since he'd retired, this was the last shred of power he had. So he held it over them. Mary didn't care. But Jezebel did.

So yes, Jezebel would be listening. And she'd be trying to pin point every little instance in which Mary fucked up, trying to find something she could drag up in front of Satan to prove Mary was unfit.

Mary pulls the headset apart so her ears can throb freely. To her right she can hear pig-woman stumbling through the script and sucking down more food.

Jezebel, the headphones whisper in her sister's faux-Southern drawl. She lets the earphones snap back in place, and a sharp sting reverberates out from her ears, reaching from the tip of her horns down to her collarbones.

"Mrs. O'Malley?" she says, before the sting has subsided. The moment she speaks, she hates it. She hates the voice she uses on customers. She hates the things she has to say. She runs the beads through her fingers, and her personal mantra through her head.

This is not my voice. These are not my words.

"Who's calling?" The voice on the other end is brittle and sexless with age.

"This is Mary. Is this Mrs. O'Malley?" Mary pinches a bead between her fingers and looks at the screen, waiting to read off the legal disclaimers she's required to tack on to the start of every call.

"I don't know any Mary," the voice is suspicious. By this point, Mary is sure it is Mrs. O'Malley, but she needs her to say so before she can start.

"I'm calling on behalf of Reverand Jezebel," Mary says. "Is this Mrs. O'Malley?"

There's a deep sigh on the other end. "Yes, I suppose it is."

"Well, Mrs. O'Malley, this is Mary. *I wanted to let you know that this call may be monitored for quality and legal purposes, and I am calling on behalf of the Jezebel Foundation.*" She spits it out in one breath and clicks over to the second page, but it's largely unnecessary. She's said all this enough that she could do it in her sleep. "First of all we wanted to thank you for all your generous support of Jezebel, and her work against the devil in the past—"

"I sent that bitch twenty dollars once. One time. And you all have been sending me postcards and calling me on the phone ever since. Why, you've probably wasted more money hounding me for cash than I gave in the first place," Mrs. O'Malley says.

Lost cause, Mary thinks. She tightens her fingers on the bead and feels the pressure of it seep through the pad of her thumb and into her bone. She has to ask anyway. Even if it will only make Mrs. O'Malley angry.

Jezebel wants them angry.

Mary pulls the mic away for a moment and covers it with her hand to let out her own sigh before she plunges back into her marketer voice—a higher, reedier version of what she really sounds like, one that makes her cringe every time she hears it played back to her.

"And we really did appreciate the support you showed, we did. First and foremost we wanted to thank you for that. If we seem eager it is only because we know you are a Good Soldier of Christ, Mrs. O'Malley, and we can depend on you to continue supporting us in the fight against Satan and his army of Sinners. So, Mrs. O'Malley, can I ask you for a generous donation of twenty dollars, as you provided before?"

"God dammit, I'm on social security, living out here alone for the past five years. I don't have the money to send to some perm-headed harlot twenty damn dollars every time she asks for it," Mrs. O'Malley says.

Mary wants to tell Mrs. O'Malley she understands what it's like to be dead broke. That she's got student loans, a worthless degree, a shit job with shit pay, and she has to live with her father. But Mrs. O'Malley doesn't care to hear that. She cares even less for what Mary does say.

"Social security isn't going to save you when the devil rises up, Mrs. O'Malley," Mary says.

This is a transition she had come up with on her own once, when she was feeling the bit of her father in her. Her managers hated it. They wanted to fire her, in fact, when they heard it. Mary was supposed to comfort the customers, sympathize with them until they handed their money over. Not threaten them. But Jezebel loved it, and insisted they let Mary slide. She had pull because she gave them money. She was, in fact, the whole reason Mary got the job. Which made Mary feel like shit.

This time, however, it wasn't the bit of the devil in her that caused her to say it, but the script. And for just a moment Mary's practiced reading voice stumbles like pig-woman's. Because the script has changed completely. This is the first time she realized, because it's the first time she's gotten this far without being cussed out or hung up on.

"What did you say to me?" Mrs. O'Malley asks. Mary can just picture her clutching her pearls and holding the phone a few inches from her face, her nose curled up like she's just found a steaming shit pile in the middle of her kitchen.

"I said—" Mary swallows and squeezes her hand shut around the beads as she looks at the new script. She doesn't want to say this to a little old church woman. She doesn't want to say it to anyone, really. But a job is a job. "Social security isn't going to save you when the devil rises up, Mrs. O'Malley. It won't keep the demons, who are even now pressing against the weak veil between their world and ours, from sinking their teeth into that greyed, wrinkled rag you call an ass. It won't keep them from tearing you apart, limb from limb from limb, slowly, while your children and your grandchildren watch. And that is just the start of what they plan to do to you, Mrs. O'Malley. And it is just a small portion of what you deserve. But we can keep it all from happening, Mrs. O'Malley. I understand that twenty dollars may be a lot, given your circumstances. How about fifteen instead?"

As she finishes the last line she closes her eyes and lets out a shuddered breath, counting the beads she blindly runs between her fingers.

1, 2, 3, 4, 5—

She hears Mrs. O'Malley snort on the other line.

"Dear," Mrs. O'Malley says. "Kindly go fuck yourself. And tell that fruity, bullshit, con-artist of a preacher to go fuck herself, too." Then Mrs. O'Malley hangs up, just as Mary decides she likes her.

For a moment Mary is hanging onto dead air, and all around her she hears the hum of her coworkers' conversations rising and falling. Some are screaming, she realizes. Sometimes this happens. Sometimes people lose it. But usually the managers swoop in immediately and put an end to it, pack up the screamer, and send them on their way. But this time, it just goes on. Below the sound, she can hear a dull thud, repeating over and over, from the direction of the office.

She checks the clock in the corner of her screen. 11:29:17. Only 43 seconds until she's sent to lunch. She leans forward and presses the rosary beads against her forehead. She thinks about praying. Praying that she doesn't get connected to another call. Praying that an earthquake hits and the whole building has to shut down. That the earth opens up and swallows the whole damned place. But she knows the man upstairs doesn't do her family any favors, and there isn't anyone below in a position to grant them.

A blue screen pops up over Mary's script. *Out to Lunch*, alongside a blinking timer counting the seconds. Mary is out of her seat before it can reach three. The man next to her watches her rise, a muffled voice barely audible over his headset.

"Fuck this," he mumbles, and clicks the disconnect button. He stands up before the lunch screen appears and catches up to Mary.

"You got a cigarette?" he asks. Mary has never seen him smoke. The pockets under his eyes are glowing with a sheen of sweat, and they look deep. Like someone pressed their thumbs into clay and leaned all the way forward. Mary chooses not to say anything, and loots her pack out of her bag to hand one over.

"Thanks," he says. "Did you know you have something growing out of your head?"

Outside the smokers' pavilion is overflowing. Usually there are just enough people that a few can't find seats, but today they are packed one next to the other like sardines, and spilling onto the lawn. Her neighbor leans against one of the wooden posts and Mary stands next to him.

"Lighter?" he asks, and she hands one over. He tucks the cigarette in his mouth, lights it, and hands it back. She does the same. From behind them the voices in the smokers' pavilion blend together into a wild hum. An animal shelter noise. Or maybe a swarm of insects. Mary closes her eyes and takes a drag off her cigarette. It tastes like sour cloth. It does little for the thrumming in her head or the feeling of pinching mouths along her body. It's warm in the sunlight. The way her sweat pools under her arms and between her thighs reminds her of when she was a child playing outside during the summer.

She used to idolize her father then. He seemed so big, and unrighteous. She used to pick sticks up off the ground as long and thick as her arm and wield them at the sky, listing off the litany of curses she'd heard her father use against the Almighty.

Someone grabs her by the back of the neck and squeezes just shy of hard. She opens her eyes and tilts her head back. Above her, a boy she almost knows from another floor is leaning against the pavilion's banister and staring down at her. He's got a face she can never put a name to. One that's too round and large for his body, which is only slightly pudgy. Typically they sit outside together in almost silence, every now and then listing an occasional grievance while they smoke. Sometimes he asks her for coffee after work. Mary always lies and says she's busy.

"Come up here," he tells her. Mary steps away from the banister and turns to look at him and the crowd. She shakes her head.

"I'm okay," she says.

He snorts. "No, you're not. You look like shit. Is this guy bugging you?" He turns towards Mary's neighbor and sneers at him. "Hey, dude. You bugging her?"

The man runs a hand through the stubble on his chin and looks at round face for just a moment. "I'm just trying to smoke. Leave me be."

"Get up here," round-face says again, and again Mary shakes her head.

"There's no room," Mary says. She looks at the grass. It's browning under the toes of her dress shoes.

You are Satan's daughter. Satan's last daughter. And you are letting this moon-face make you uncomfortable. You could tear his skin off in one fluid yank and make a bathrobe out of it. Your father would be proud. Prouder of you than he's ever been of Jezebel and her designer blazers and overdone hair.

This is not my voice. These are not my words.

Mary's stomach wilts. She squats on the ground and puts a hand to her forehead so the beads dangle against her face. She feels the edge of her horn, and presses a palm against it. It's hot and vibrating.

"You want to go somewhere else?" Round-face asks. He squirms against the people behind him until he can get a leg over the banister. Then another. He lands on his knees on the other side and reaches towards Mary. "We could go to the bathroom together."

"Man, can't you see she's not in the mood for your shit," Mary's neighbor snaps. "Get the fuck out of here."

"Fuck you, man." Round-face wraps a hand around the banister and pulls himself to his feet. "No one's talking to you."

"Well, I'm talking to you." For a moment they stand chest to chest, and Mary watches them from the ground. She can feel bile in her throat. But she also feels heat pulsing in her groin and spreading through her chest. She swallows a mouthful of saliva.

"You looking for sloppy seconds or some shit," round-face says.

"I will slap the teeth right out of your mouth today. Don't push me." Her neighbor tosses the cigarette to the ground and lifts his chin. He has at least a foot on round-face, and both have realized it.

"What the fuck ever, man," round-face says. He shrugs his shoulders and strides past Mary towards the building. "Like she's even worth it."

Both Mary and her neighbor watch him go. When Mary stands, flashes of color eat away at her vision. When the door closes she looks to her neighbor. She knows she should say something. He looks at her, frowning.

"I hope whoever's up there forgives us for what we've done," he says. Then he turns away from Mary and walks towards the parking lot. Mary watches him get in a car and drive away. When he's gone, she walks along the side of the building and heads in. For the most part the cubicles are all still empty. Most of the representatives are still outside. Mary can see them through the windows milling around the smoker's pavilion, or meandering through the parking lot. Those at their desks are either screaming into their mics, or sitting slumped back in their seats staring at nothing. A manager is circulating around the floor, but he's not doing much other than clapping the occasional shoulder of a representative in a congratulatory way. On his cheek and down the left breast of his shirt, there's a smear of something dark and tacky.

Mary sits next to pig-woman, who is still on the mic. Along her desk there are crumpled up plastic bags and an array of crumbs. This is normal. It's so normal it makes Mary dizzy. Pig-woman pulls the headphones off her ears and looks at Mary with wide eyes.

"The man on the other line just keeps wailing," she says. "You think I should hang up? I don't want to get in trouble."

"Did you ask them to donate?" Mary asks. Pig-woman nods. "Twice?" Mary asks. Pig-woman nods. "Then just hang up."

"Are you sure?" Pig-woman asks, covering her mic.

"I don't think anyone really gives a fuck, to be honest with you,"

Mary says. Pig-woman gapes at her then looks up towards where the manager is strolling.

"Don't cuss. You could get *fired*," pig-woman whispers.

"Just hang up on the guy already, and mind your own business," Mary pushes the headset over her ears, and logs in. As the prompt loads she takes a bead between her fingers. Her nails, she notices, have hardened. The tips are blackening.

I am becoming, she thinks. She looks out the window and sees two of her coworkers wrestling against the banister of the smoking pavilion. The rest are gathered around, their mouths moving rapidly.

We are becoming, Mary thinks again. It's not her voice. Nor is it the voice she uses on customers. It's more like a voice from deep in her guts and groin. Like if her cunt could talk, she thinks. It's the same voice that told her to skin round-face.

The headset connects to a call, and she hears the voice again, this time it whispers out of the headset.

Jezebel.

On the other end there is nothing but the sound of sirens in the distance. Mary hears a hiccup, and a low moan.

"Keep smiling, keep dialing folks," the manager calls from the other end of the room. "Good job today, people. Good job."

"Hello?" Mary asks into the mic.

The other end gurgles and Mary disconnects. The next call there's a woman laughing. Hysterically, the way Mary thought only bad actors in B-movies laughed. She hears an infant crying, just audible under the laughter.

"Hello?" Mary says.

"Hello?" It's a whispered voice. A child's voice. "Is this the doctor?"

"No," Mary says. "It's not."

"We need help," the child says. "Can you—"

"No, sorry." Mary says, and hangs up. She licks cold sweat off her lip and pulls the headset off. She hits the Away From Desk button. She doesn't wait to see if her request is granted or not. Pig-woman looks at her as she stands up.

"Feeling sick," Mary says. "I got to go call my dad."

Mary heads to the bathroom, pressing the beads against her stomach, her head, her lips. In the women's room someone has smeared lipstick across the mirror. There are handprints. Crude drawings. The toilet paper is unrolled from several stalls and strewn across the room, over the sinks, and tops of the cubicles, to hang like streamers. In the last stall the door is closed, and Mary can hear someone crying softly and whispering. She goes into the first and locks the door. She squats with her feet on the lid and rests her head on her knees.

She calls her father's number.

"Hello?" her father yells, his voice echoing over the phone lines. "Who's this?" There's a pause where she hears the phone shift. "Mary? Is that you?"

"Yeah," Mary says.

"Aren't you at work?" he asks.

"I'm not feeling well," Mary says. She rips some toilet paper apart that's hanging nearby and presses it to her wet face then blows her nose, and wads it into a ball.

"What's wrong, sweetie?" Satan asks, his voice dropping low and softening.

"I don't know. I just don't feel good at all," Mary says. She bites her knuckle and a small animal noise escapes around it.

"You want me to come get you?" Satan asks. "Me and Jezebel will come get you." Mary hears Satan breathe in deep, and then bellow for Jezebel twice in a row.

"No, no. Not Jezebel. She'll be mad," Mary says. "I'm on her file."

"Nonsense, she won't be mad. Whatever she's got going on isn't more important than her sister. She'll understand," Satan says, then bellows for Jezebel once more.

"Dad," Mary says, leaning back against the back of the toilet and looking up at the canopy of paper. "You should just give hell to Jezebel. She wants it. And she's better than me. I can't make you proud, Dad. But she can." Mary snatches more toilet paper and blows her nose into it until she can hear the hollow whoosh of air streaming in to fill her emptying sinuses.

"Mary," Satan says. "You're talking crazy. Jezebel isn't—"

Mary hears the snap of Jezebel's heels in the background. "What is it?" Jezebel asks.

"It's Mary, she says she's not feeling well. We should go get her," Satan says. There's a shuffle on the other line, and then Satan's voice, muffled but still talking, fades into the distance.

"Hello? Mary?" Jezebel says into the phone. "I got this, Dad. You should just go take a nap or something. You need rest. Mary, what are you doing? You should be on the clock."

"I don't feel good," Mary says. Mary hears the jingle of Jezebel's earrings on the other end, and correctly assumes she's rolling her eyes.

"Well no shit, Mary," Jezebel says. "Do you think life is about feeling good? 'Cause I got news for you, kiddo, it's not. In all those years spent studying those smarty-pants dead white men you never learned that? Nobody feels good. The point of life is not to feel good. It's to buckle down and do the work you need to do."

"I want to talk to Dad," Mary says.

"Why would you want to talk to him? Mary, what can he do for you? What has he done? For either of us? He was never going to hand over hell, you know. Not to you or me. The whole reason hell even became a thing was cause he was pissed his daddy was showing attention to someone else, so he threw a hissy fit. Now he's just holding Hell over our heads hoping to get our attention. Hoping we throw the same fit. He'll never just hand the keys over. He'll wait till we die, then move back into Hell, and go through the motions till he fathers a few more kids and starts the whole game over again. I've figured it out, Mary. You ought to have, too," Jezebel says, and in between the spaces of her words Mary can hear her nails rap against a hard surface, one after the other, like falling rain.

"Please just let me talk to Dad," Mary says.

"He's old news, Mary. Hell is old news. He can keep it. I'm making my own place here on Earth. I'm doing what he never could. Never had the nerve to. If you play your cards right, you might just find yourself a place there, Mary. But you got to get back on those phones, and Do. Your. Job. Do you understand? And if you see the sword, don't touch it. Just call me."

There's a click, and the call goes dead. Mary sits on the toilet and lights a cigarette. She sits there, smoking, until her breath evens out. She goes to the sink and washes her face. On either side of her head her horns stand, thick and long as her forearm. Looking at them makes her back ache. Jezebel's, when they've grown in, are only ever nubs. Cute, little and goat like. Her father is always complimenting Mary's horns, but Mary still envies Jezebel's.

Mary steps out of the bathroom, and something grabs the back of her neck and pushes her against the wall. Presses up against her body. Something is wedged painful and stiff into the small of her back.

"You want to fuck?" someone asks, wet and hot in her ear, and so close she can feel the tip of the tongue brush her lobe.

She shoves herself off the wall hard enough to knock them back a step. She squeezes out from under their arms and thinks Run, but instead she turns to look. It's round-face. Sweaty, and for some reason, shirtless.

"Come on," he says. "We could just pop into the bathroom."

She slaps him across the face, and her nails leave three deep gorges flanked by two thin red lines across his cheek to the edge of his lip. It feels like lightning goes through her wrist, down her spine and into her belly when she makes contact. She nearly swings on him again, but instead pulls her hand to her chest and cradles it there.

"You bitch," he moans. "You frigid, stuck-up cunt." He spits on her, and turns to run down the hall.

Mary lights another cigarette and smokes it right there, looking at her nails. They're hard as wood now. Underneath, there's small off-white balls of round-face skin wedged up against her fingers. She puts her tongue to one and tastes salted meat.

She goes back in the bathroom to wash her hands and flush the cigarette down the toilet. Then she returns to the floor.

Pig-woman is gazing out the window when Mary gets back. She follows her eyes and sees a flock of representatives on the lawn. Many have stripped their clothes off. Some are tangled in the limbs of each other. Fighting or fucking, it's hard to tell the difference. There are some that are covered in blood. There's someone hanging from the inside rafters of the smoking pavilion.

"Somethings wrong," pig-woman says to Mary. Mary looks at her. Takes in pig-woman's dopey eyes, her apple cheeks, her stubbed nose. The bags of chips on the counter and the crumbs scattered on the crotch of her pants.

She's the best of all of us, Mary thinks. The thought knocks the wind out of her, and there's an ache in Mary's chest she can't explain. *You've got to be kidding me. Here is human goodness, embodied. A spirit strong enough to withstand the temptations of the devil. Blessed are the humble.*

Mary wants to snort and cry.

"You should go home to your kids, or something," Mary says.

Pig-woman looks unsure, as if she's going to ask if it's okay. "What about you?" she asks instead.

"I'll be fine," Mary says. Pig-woman looks at her for a moment, but only a moment, before she grabs her purse from below her desk and heads for the door without logging out.

Mary puts her headphones back on. She has to tilt them back so that they sit on her head at the right angle. On the monitor, it shows a call is already connected.

"Hello?" Mary asks. "Mrs. Connors?"

There's nothing but fuzz. Mary thinks of hanging on to this call. Of just staying on the line and giving her pitch to dead air, over and over. It'd be a way to spite Jezebel without Mary having to actually take a stand.

"Mrs. Connors?" Mary says again, and begins to doubt her plan would work. Jezebel would hear the silence on the other end, and she'd know. She'd know her sister was a coward. But that was something she already knew. It's something she had always known.

She glides her cursor over to the disconnect button when there's a small scrape and hiccup on the other end.

"Dear? Hello?"

Mary feels her heart sting a little. Satan's daughters are often called many things, but dear is hardly ever among them. They can be baby, they can be sweetie, they can be honey, but they are never dear.

"Mrs. Connors?" Mary asks.

"Oh, I thought you might be my daughter," she said. "I was hoping you were my daughter. That's why I stayed—but you aren't are you? I better let you go. She might be calling now." The voice is soft the way that old couches get soft when they're well used, and damp the way that voices get damp when there've been tears.

"Mrs. Connors, I'm calling on behalf of Reverend Jezebel," Mary says.

"I'm sorry, dear. So sorry. But I don't have time to talk. My daughter might be calling. She may be ringing right now," Mrs. Connors says, and Mary can hear that she is sorry, and Mary feels sorry, too.

"Ma'am, we wanted to ask you—"

"You've already called three times today. You called and my husband answered and then he said the most terrible things to me. Things you would never imagine a person saying. He slit his own throat, after. I've been calling my daughter all day. I've been waiting for her to call back, but it's only ever you people. I'm sorry. But I don't have time for this. Something is going wrong. So wrong." At the end of this, Mrs. Connors lets out a little shuddered breath, but she doesn't sob.

"It has, Mrs. Connor. And I'm sorry for it."

There's a tremor through the earth. Mary feels it shake through the floor and up into the seat. It travels up her spine and into her horns, and for a moment her whole body is a vibration both sweet and painful. Under the smoking pavilion fissures open up in the ground and split apart. There's a pulsating, red glow seeping out from under the earth. In the office things begin to crash to the floor, then it stills for a moment.

Mary takes a deep breath and pinches one of the beads between her fingers. It begins to sizzle, then grow bright orange and white in her fingertips before it dissolves into nothing but ash. The string snaps and the necklace falls limp, all the beads scattering to the floor.

"Dear, are you alright?" Mrs. Connors ask.

"I'm fine," Mary says. "It was just an earthquake."

"Where are you?" Mrs. Connor asks, concerned. "Was it bad? Are you hurt? Is anyone hurt?"

"I'm in Ohio, ma'am." Mary looks out the window, where earth is steadily falling into the fissures and lava is slowly rising up. Some of the representatives have caught fire, but they're still moving, still fighting, still fucking, as if nothing has changed. She can see charred skeletons with their mouths flapping open and shut in laughter. "Everyone's fine, Mrs. Connors. Thank you for asking."

"We live down in Florida, you know," Mrs. Connors says. "We moved here after our girl got married and Albert retired. Came down from Minnesota about five or six years ago. You know, the weather is lovely. A little hot maybe. Humid in the summers, I think. They're still hard to bear even after all these years. But it's good for Albert's arthritis. Even so, I'm a Northern girl at heart, you know. Always probably will be. I miss the winter sometimes. And I miss my daughter. She's probably calling now."

Mary knows Mrs. Connors` daughter will never call. She can see her, spending the end of days alone in a shabby condo for seniors, waiting with her husband's dead body by the phone for a call that will never come. The same way she hopes her father's sitting by the window, watching the sky turn to ash and soot, and wondering when Mary'll come home.

Outside a pit has opened wide enough to swallow the whole pavilion and the representatives who weren't quick enough to get out of the way. From within the pit Mary can see black twisted things making their way up the walls claw by claw. Things she remembers from her childhood, before her father retired and moved them up to the surface. Because Hell is no place to raise your daughters. At least, not if you love them. And Satan did love them, in his way. At least Mary hopes so.

There's a tremor on the other end of the line, and Mary hears a crash. Glass breaking. Mrs. Connors gives a gasp and Mary hears a soft thud, like a bag of wet laundry hitting the floor, followed by the clatter of plastic, louder and more distinct.

"Mrs. Connors?" Mary asks. Her voice echoes back at her. "Mrs. Connors, are you alright?"

There's no sound on the other end of the line. The sky is opaque. The lot lights have come on, but their shine is dull, as if obscured by a curtain. Most of the light comes from the abyss that opened beneath the smoking pavilion, and even that's not great. Mary can no longer tell which shapes skittering through the grass are representatives, and which are things that crawled out of the pit.

Her cellphone vibrates in her pocket, and she wrestles it out. *Jezebel*.

Mary sends it to voicemail.

"Mrs. Connors?" Mary asks again. There is something like a wheeze over the line.

Her phone buzzes with a message from Jezebel. *Call me.*

Outside the pit glows and the lot lights flicker, and there is another rumble. Above, there is a bright spot burning through the clouds. There is something living in Mary's head, some desperate starved thing, trying to beat its way out.

She can barely manage to type with her nails this long. *On a call. Dad okay?*

CALL ME.

"Mrs. Connors?" Mary asks, and thinks about looking up her donor information. So maybe she can call an ambulance. So she can do something to feel less powerless. But she knows there are no ambulances, and she has no power. She never did.

The bright spot burns through the clouds and becomes a shaft of light, so bright Mary can't look at it head on. Its edges sparkle with iridescent glitter. Some poor thing gets caught in the beam of it. Its body shoots upright and it begins to claw at its own skin. To shriek, wail and writhe. Then, blindly, it turns and runs towards the call center, and smacks into the window. The face is twisted, and mostly unrecognizable now. The eyes have bulged, and there's pockets of pus all along its forehead and down the bridge of its nose. But Mary recognizes the three gorges in its round cheek.

The face splits in two against the window. The body slumps downward. Behind it is a being that seems made entirely of blue skies, sunlight, and clouds, wielding a sword that's made of gold.

From within the shaft of light, more of these beings are descending. And from behind the clouds, more shafts of light are breaking free and touching down. The beams widen, and Mary can see the dark things on the ground skitter away from them, and crane their jointed necks upward to gawk. When the blue sky beings touch down, there is an immediate fray of bodies coming together.

There's another rumble. From where the smoking pavilion stood lava is rising up, pouring off a hefty rectangle slab that is pushing its way out of the Earth.

Her phone buzzes again. *Dad.*

Mary takes the earphone off one ear and puts her own phone there.

"Hello? Dad?"

"Is the sword there?" Jezebel asks. "Is it there?"

"Where's Dad?"

"Don't touch it, Mary. I'm telling you right now. Do. Not. Lay. A. Fucking. Finger. On. It. Or I will kill you, Mary. I don't want to, but I will. I'll have to. Is the sword there?"

"Hello?" Mary hears distantly through the headphone. She hangs up on Jezebel.

"Mrs. Connors?" she asks.

There's the sound of cloth brushing wood, and weakly, again: "Hello?"

Outside the angels, because what else could they be, are pouring over the parking lot, skewering this and that. Some angels are overwhelmed by bodies. Blood red bodies, pale fleshy bodies, bodies with many joints. But for every one that falls there are five more that come down. And it's clear there's no direction on the other side. No leadership. No clear sense of where to go. Mary watches some representatives—or maybe demons—make breaks towards the end of the parking lot, only to be run down.

The lava stops flowing as the slab fully emerges. Then, as if the whole thing were one large candle, a fire sparks up top. In place of the wick, there's a sword. As tall as Jezebel, who is a good foot taller than Mary, and as thick as Mary's thighs, which are double the size of Jezebel's. It burns black at the center, like blood clotting in a deep wound. Like hell.

I could take that, Mary thinks. *I could take that, and be commander of hell. I could kill Jezebel. I could stop all this. Or take it all over. Be a stronger Satan. A gentler God. And Dad—he would be proud, wouldn't he? He'd be proud enough to love me.*

Isn't that all anyone wants? Isn't that why he went to war in the first place?

"Hello? Is that you, baby girl?" It's Mrs. Connors in her ear again, but it's also her father's voice. Weak with age and trembling with fright. "Hello?"

Her phone buzzes. *Jezebel.*

"Hello," Mary says, dropping her customer service voice. "Can you hear me?"

"Baby girl?" Mrs. Connors asks. "Elizabeth, is that you?"

"Yeah, Mom. It's me."

"It's been so long, I hardly recognize your voice," Mrs. Connors says.

Outside there are more bright spots burning in the clouds.

Above the sword, there's one asteroid-sized light burning the atmosphere into a shimmering haze. When she looks at the sword, Mary feels a hook right under her navel trying to reel her towards it.

Her body says *mine*.

Her body says *become*.

This is not my voice, these are not my words, Mary thinks, and reaches for beads that are no longer there.

"I know," Mary says. "I'm sorry, Mom."

"I'm glad you're calling now, dear," Mrs. Connors says. "Things have gotten—well, are you alright?"

The sky is splitting. More angels. More aching light. More buzzing phone. And all the while her skull is pounding, *let me out, let me out*, and the representatives and demons are wailing, and the swords is calling her body *mine mine mine*, and her father, how is her father? Does he feel it, too? The itching fire in his veins? That his skin is too tight? Is he scared? Is he alone?

Or is he clapping Jezebel on the back? Is he looking at her with proud tears in his eyes?

I'll kill you, Mary-

Or is he dead?

"I'm alright," Mary says. "Thank you fo—thanks, Mom. Are you alright?"

"I think I took a tumble," Mrs. Connors says. "I think I fell down. I don't want to worry you though, dear. It's just—it's dark here, and I'm a little confused. It's so dark. And things are so strange."

The bright patch above the sword finishes burning a hole in the sky. It's no beam of light coming through. Something else is emerging. Something that looks like thunder given flesh.

"I don't want to trouble you, dear," Mrs. Connors says. "But do you think—would you mind—coming to see me, soon?"

Is lying inherently evil? Is anyone inherently evil? What is evil and what isn't? Mary went to school to learn these things, and came out knowing nothing for certain.

Come home, baby girl.

"It's no trouble," Mary says, and she reaches up to rub the length of her horns, which are sore. Which are vibrating. "I'm actually headed your way right now. I wanted to surprise you. I'm almost there. Just lay down and take a nap, and I'll be there by the time you open your eyes."

Out of the hole a finger has emerged, now two, now three. The clouds crackle with electricity where they brush against the appendages, and then burn away into light. Each finger must be the size of a skyscraper. Or maybe even larger. Here's four. And now the thumb.

Everything on the ground stills as they look up at the palm descending. The air grows heavy. The building begins to shake, and Mary hears bursts of static coursing through her headphones. It eats something Mrs. Connors says, and the signal grows faint.

"Mrs. Connors?" Mary says, and there's another burst of static.

"—dear?"

"I'm sorry, Mom" Mary says. "Bad connection. What did you say?"

The phone buzzes. The phone buzzes. The palm descends.

"I said I love you, dear."

Mary looks up at the palm. She imagines herself, standing before it with a stick raised. Her father with the sword in one hand, his other hand spread across the crown of her head. She imagines them there together, standing against the insurmountable fury of God.

"I love you, too," she says.

The building continues to shake, and Mary hears Mrs. Connors take a breath in before a definite click kills the connection. A wave of white noise follows. Her name plate rattles off the top of her cubicle and bounces to the floor.

She sits back, listening to dead air, as the hand makes contact. First with the hilt of the sword, which crumbles like tinfoil. Then the fingers curl downward and it starts to tear through the roof of the building. Mary tilts her head back and lets the headset slip off her ears. She closes her eyes and breathes in, holds the breath, waiting.

She feels a gentle, cleansing burn spread across her, like when her father dabbed her scrapes with rubbing alcohol. She lets go of her phone. It falls among the spilled beads. She lets go of her horns and her skin as the heat of the hand begins to burn them away. She lets her breath go in one long, shuddering sob.

Mary lets go.

She lets it all go.

The Woman the Spiders Loved

There was a woman who the spiders fell in love with. You knew her in high school, but you weren't friends. She was plainish. She still is.

But that didn't matter to the spiders. They thought she was beautiful. It was something about her hair. It's long. She's never cut it, and it's very blonde. A spider saw her waiting for the bus one day, and it fell in love just as it was laying its eggs. When its young hatched and ate their mother's corpse, they also ate that love.

They lived in her house under her bed. When she slept, they would slink out from underneath and do small things to let her know how much they loved her. No, they didn't write messages in webs. This is not a children's story. They didn't lay eggs in her skin, either, so don't ask.

They kissed her. With their little pincers, they nipped her skin inch after inch. She woke up itching every morning, covered in small angry welts. Her skin was always speckled with tight black scabs from where she scratched the bites open with her nails. When the scabs fell off the spiders collected them. They tied them up in their silk ropes, and hung them like chandeliers from the underside of her bed. They went on biting, and she went on scratching. The spiders weren't poisonous enough to kill her, but each night she got a little more numb, until she could hardly feel anything at all.

One day she called the exterminator, and the house was filled with gas. The spiders all died. She swept the remains out from under her bed, along with the small altars they had built from her skin. After that, no one ever loved her like the spiders did. In fact, no one ever loved her at all. She went on not feeling, and the spiders went on not living.

That's just the way it is with love sometimes, I guess.

Miloslav

You may think you know a lot more about the world and how it works than I do. You don't have to lie, I can read it in everything you do. From the very way you part your hair to the way your pinky toe curls whenever my mouth opens. I`m not dumb, despite what you think. I'd wager I'm a whole lot smarter than you in some ways. In the ways that really matter, you know, when it comes to being human. Like for instance, I bet you ain't ever seen a bear O.D. Go ahead and roll your eyes, but there's a lot you can learn from that. At least there was when it was the bear that I knew.

I met him while I was doing grunt-level carnie work in my mid-twenties. He was a dancing bear, snatched by some carnival hippies when he was just a wee-thing. Then those carnie-hippies slapped insult right on top of injury by naming him Miloslav. He wasn't even from Russia--they caught him in the Northern part of Canada. But they turned him right into a stereotype. The Russian Dancing Bear. Not even just any old stereotype, but a Commie stereotype at that. You know in general America ain`t got too many kind words for Commies. Even the most reasonable and level headed of people have been known to pop off when they hear the word "comrade" uttered anywhere on their block. Imagine how the average *rural*—and by rural, I mean backwater shithole--carnival-going American would treat someone with the name Miloslav. Someone wearing a jaunty little red cap and matching vest. Now imagine if that someone was also a bear, who didn`t have the education or the verbal ability to defend himself.

Shiiiit.

Miloslav had a hard life, you see what I'm saying? I know *I* see what I'm saying just fine. After all, you know I ain't a stranger to hard knocks. If my life had a face, its nose would look more rocky mountain ridge than gentle slope, and it'd only be able to chew with one side of its mouth. But compared to Miloslav? My life looks like Ms. Universe. Or at the very least Ms. Kentucky.

I digress. You know all about my life and its many *issues*, as you call 'em. What you need to hear about now is Miloslav.

Miloslav grew up in the last true carnival—the kind with freaks, geeks, animal cruelty and human rights violations galore—that kept itself under-wraps and afloat by going to places where those things appealed to the population at large. The folks that snatched him raised and trained him. He was scared at first, for sure, and confused. But young enough to adapt and most importantly, to bury. For a while he just let himself forget all about the woods, and his mother, and assumed that he was the same thing as the humans who toted him around in a baby-seat and taught him to dance. You might think it's ridiculous Miloslav ever confused himself for a human child, but at that particular carnival lots of parents spent their time nurturing their children by screaming things like, "One two three—dip—bend—No!—Dip! You stupid animal!" The only difference in Miloslav's eyes was that he had a lot more hair, a lot sharper nails, and the other children would talk to each other, but not to him. In fact, whenever he came near, they all ran off as quick as they could.

But the adults were even worse. When Miloslav did perform, no matter how well he did, and let me tell you there isn't a dancer out there like Miloslav, but we'll get to that later, they chucked all sorts of nasty shit at him. Old banana peels slimy with mold and rot. Used up diapers. Even rocks, sometimes, the bastards. Miloslav was an easy target. Because he was different. Or maybe because he was beautiful. Maybe those two things are the same thing. Regardless, the backwater hicks the carnival catered to hated him. And they loved to hate him. He made his kidnappers rich by getting pelted with trash and demeaned for years. Insult on top of injury on top of insult on top of shit. That was Miloslav's life.

Never had a true parent, a lover, or even a friend. You can imagine how lonely he was by the time he neared the end of his adolescence, which is right about the time I met him and started cleaning his tent after his performances. It was a shit job, but I wasn't a pretty enough girl to work the rides, or try to hook people into winning prizes, and the top-carnie said I wasn't strong enough to do maintenance. That tent stank to high hell, let me tell you what. And I'd leave every night eyes watering and nose plugged with mucus. But not just because of the stench. But because of Miloslav. Because of the way he moved. Nothing makes art like pain. And while a three-hundred-pound brown bear shouldn't be able to pluck sound from the air the way birds grab hold of the wind with their wings, that's exactly what Miloslav did. Shit you not.

I used to stand in the back and watch as he danced through the torrent of trash and think I was the only one who gave a damn about that bear's performance. When I watched him I felt something. Right up next to my heart. Like there was something stirring there, trying to wake up after a long nap. Trying to break its way out. Like maybe a bird, testing the bars of its cage. But nobody else ever seemed to feel that way. It was a shame. Seeing him dance like that and as well as he did, I had to wonder what it would be like if he weren't getting pegged in the head with something putrid every thirty seconds. But I ain't ever say anything. You know as well as I do, I ain't exactly a hero, now am I? I didn't do anything but stand back and watch. Maybe every now and then I'd offer Miloslav a nip off a bottle of something-something at the end of my shift, and sit with him for a little, talking in our little, small way. You could get to understand him, see--if you spent the time. But there wasn't a soul willing to spend the time except me. And there wasn't a soul that appreciated his dance except me. Or at least that's what I thought.

Then one night a pretty young blonde girl threw her hands up and stormed to the center of the ring and stood in front of Miloslav, in between him and the ruddy-face drunks and their trash.

"You stop what you're doing right now," she shouted. "You ought to be ashamed."

She went to go on, but the crowd let out one great jeer and I closed my eyes, knowing enough about what was gonna happen to not need to see it. There was a sound like a heavy hail storm, and some cuss words thrown out that would make me on even my very worst days blush and apologize. When the laughter died down and was replaced by the tromp of feet fading into the distance, I opened my eyes again, and that pretty blonde girl was standing knee-deep in a pile of garbage, her hair mussed, her skin smudged, and her eyes wet with tears. She started shaking and biting her lip.

"Bunch of ingrates." she said, "bunch of know-nothing, selfish pricks."

Miloslav was standing behind her, his arm drawn over his head and his foot stuck up straight behind him, paused in the middle of the move she'd interrupted. There was a look on his face. One that even back then I'd seen enough on others to know it meant trouble. It's the same kind of look we used to give each other not so long ago. Before you just started looking at me like I was some kind of bug.

Miloslav had tried to help the girl clean up, but his claws were useless at delicate, minute, practical work, so I ended up doing it. Once she was mostly garbage free, she sat outside the tent with me and Miloslav while we took pulls of a bottle of whiskey.

"It's not right what they do to you," she told Miloslav. "I came here 'cause I heard they had a dancing bear--which is just cruel--but then to just let people pelt you with trash on top of it?"

What do you mean? Miloslav said. In his way. With his eyes and a subtle tilt of his head, twitch of his nose, and curl of his lip. *I like to dance.*

"He says he likes to dance," I said.

"Don't play with me," she said.

"He said he likes to dance."

"But—all those people throwing things—I mean—it can't be *enjoyable*." She reached up and dabbed her trash-soaked hair behind her ear and pulled a face.

Miloslav looked at the girl. He looked at the girl in a way that made me want to get to my feet and start screaming "Fire." Start screaming "Run." Start screaming "Miloslav, you idiot, ain't you got enough pain in your life?" Start screaming anything. I was smart, back then. Smarter than I am now, that's for sure. Smarter by a mile.

Miloslav set his nose and ears to twitching.

"He says if you love something it doesn't matter if it hurts. If you love it, it makes all the pain worthwhile. If you love it, you do it, even if it pains you," I told the girl, and even as I was saying the words the girl was looking past me, looking at Miloslav, and starting to smile, and on the inside I was going *fuck fuck fuck fuck fuck*.

"Do you think we could learn to talk?" the girl asked Miloslav. "Like you two do?"

Miloslav's eyes watered and he licked his jaws.

Sometimes I lay awake while you're sleeping and wonder what would have happened if I had stepped up, stepped between Miloslav and the garbage. If right now I would have my face pressed into a coat of matted bear fur instead of turned towards a bare wall. If we'd be sleeping somewhere in a carnival tent, or if we would have went up North and found a cave in the woods where he should have been all along. It seems possible, now that I know everything that I know, that me and Miloslav are two halves of the same fool. We fell for the same honey-trap, after all.

But what if we'd been the honey for each other? What if love wasn't something that made you sick? What if I loved someone who loved back? What would it be like, if Miloslav were still alive and dancing?

I wonder that. All the time, anymore.

<3

She came by every night the week we were in that town. When we were moving on, I was excited. Figured that would be the end of me having to teach her each little twitch and turn of Miloslav's words. But then she showed up in the next town, and the town after. Until she'd been following us for two months, and they were talking just as easy as Miloslav and I ever did.

Why'd she do it? Well, I guess it made her feel good about herself, alleviating the loneliness of a poor unfortunate. It is a good feeling, isn't it? And I guess I could forgive that, if that's as far as it went.

But she didn't have to do what she did after it was clear it'd went too far. When Miloslav laid his paw on her leg and looked up at her Barbie doll face and said *I love you*, she coulda walked, and it would have been more forgivable that way. To just say well, sorry and so long. Imagine how much softer the world would be if people were that kind of honest that early.

But instead she thought she had to give him some kind of hope or something.

"Oh, Miloslav," she cooed. "I love you dearly. But we can't be together. You aren't human."

How not? What does it take? To be human?

"Well—" she said, twirling Miloslav's hair around her fingers.

I'll do it. I'll do anything.

What's it take? To be human?

That's something people with soft hands and long beards argue over all the time. Before I never cared much to think about it. All Id, no Ego, that's what you're always saying about me, right? But

I've seen what asking that question can get you, and I should have learned the first time.

What does it take to be human? Love? A code of ethics? A sense of self?

No.

A job. A state issued driver's license. Good credit. A roof and some walls and a bed that doesn't sit directly on the floor. You have to wear clothes. You have to trade passion for profession. Love for low-interest rates. Soul for safety.

That's what it takes to be human.

At least according to Miloslav's bride-to-be. You two would make a pair, I think. Fit for Better Homes and Gardens.

Miloslav shaved off his hair and started bathing first. He shivered whenever he was outside, and his flesh looked like raw chicken. There was something new, and skeletal about him that made his dancing--while still beautiful--so painful to watch that no one bothered throwing anything. But that didn't matter, because soon, Miloslav gave up dancing.

"Humans don't turn things they love into jobs," his bride-to-be said. "At least, none that go anywhere further in the world than dumps like this."

But I like to dance, Miloslav said.

"That's what weekends are for, darling," she said.

So Miloslav went into the city, dressed in a button-up shirt and a pair of uncomfortable trousers that I had to help tailor to his bear-body, and searched out a job. Low-level, office work. The bare-minimum enough to be human, I guess. He came back, smiling at me, the tie cutting deep into the waddle of his neck.

She says humans smile.

"Not the one's round here," I said, and spat into the dirt.

That night I felt Miloslav leaving. Felt it in my fingers and my toes and all the areas in between, too. I knew my almost-friend was gonna pass on into some beige afterlife where there'd be no music to carry him through the utter garbage that was the world. I'd close my eyes and all I'd think of was Miloslav dancing his way through the garbage, looking more complete and more real than any desk jockey I'd had the sour displeasure of meeting.

That night, Miloslav ransacked the trailer where his carnie-hippie kidnappers lived. He stole all their money and valuables while they slept, zonked out on whatever was their medication of choice for the evening. And then he set off to earn his bride-to-be's love.

Did I get out of bed? Did I try to go and talk sense into him?

No. I rolled over and closed my eyes harder. I ignored that feeling in my chest--the feeling of the bird, its wings, the fluttering—shut it right down and turned towards the wall, and just thought about how horrible the world is.

I think about that a lot, anymore.

It was over two years later that I saw Miloslav again. I'd left the carnival by that point and was delivering frozen slabs of meat to local grocery stores in the late nights. The stink wasn't so different from the carnival, and it followed me home at the end of every shift. But at least I had a home that wasn't a pup tent. I was on my way to becoming a legit human, I guess. Just like Miloslav. One of the stores I delivered to was this corner shit-shack in the middle of a bad neighborhood. The kind of neighborhood that only got more lively the longer the night hours wore on.

When I saw him it took me a moment to recognize him. There

were lots of bumbling rag-piles of people in that area, and so his vast, strange shape didn't seem as out of place as it might elsewhere. What initially made me look again was the quality of the clothes--he was in a blazer and a button up, and that was what set him apart. On that second look I knew instantly; that was Miloslav, the dancer. Talking to two teenish white boys in wife-beaters and oil-stained jeans, who stood on those corners all the time, palming people little bags of noxious shit.

What would Miloslav be doing in that neighborhood talking to them?

He caught the smell of meat on me and turned his head to look, nose twitching.

"Ou?" he grunted.

"Miloslav," I said.

"Ate a mhin-not," he said, then turned back to the boys, blocking whatever they were doing with his body. Then he turned back towards me. "Oo 'ou half rhyme?"

"You don't have to talk to me like that, Miloslav," I said, shrugging.

Do you have time? he asked.

I was on the clock for another two deliveries, technically. But it wasn't like I had a tracker on my ankle or anything. I know you probably don't think it was the right thing to do. But it was Miloslav, and in the two years since I'd seen him, I'd yet to make anything as close to a friend as he was. And it looked like the years had chewed on him. He was still bald, but the skin was no longer soft and bumpy as raw chicken breast. It had coarsened and tanned, like someone had plopped him down in a pan and cooked him far too long. And the flesh drooping below his eyes may as well have been hammocks, it was so loose.

Anyhow, I figured if he was on that corner talking to them boys, he was a man—or a bear—in need of someone—anyone—friendly to talk to. I knew there'd probably be consequences. But hey, that's what you do for others right? Suffer the consequences when they need you to? Ain't that what makes us human? No?

We hunkered down over a forty each on the curb of a dead end by the closed down railroad.

"Miloslav, you look like shit," I said.

You too, he said.

"But not as bad as you," I said, then took a draw off my beer. "How's the wife?"

Miloslav breathed in so hard his bear-chest, skeletal though it was, near burst out of his button-up.

Love is a thing, he said.

"I guess so," I said.

Love is a thing I don't understand. It's a cruel thing, he said.

I considered my beer. I took another long drag. "Yep," I said.

It's the only thing I care about in the world, Miloslav said.

"Are you going to tell me what's up or not?"

And so Miloslav told me.

Miloslav had gotten the job. He had gotten the apartment. He had gotten a bed that the girl would lay in, with him, back to back. She gave him kisses on the forehead. She packed his lunch for work. In the evening they would sit and she would put her feet in his lap while they watched whatever flickered across the small TV in their living room. On weekends he would dance for her to the radio. Dance with her. And she would feel so small and perfect in his arms, and her mouth would open wide enough to swallow the whole of his heart, and Miloslav thought this was it, this was being human, this was enough.

But it wasn't. It never is, is it? It's only ever enough for now with some people.

Soon enough she was upset all the time. The space was too small. The food was too cheap. The neighbors down the way not clean or quiet or right enough. Walking everywhere was tiresome. His dancing was boring. His claws were too sharp. She needed more. More room. More things. More time alone.

Miloslav started filing his claws down. He started putting in more hours at the job. He got another job to work on weekends. Eventually he was making enough to rent a house—one that he was hardly ever at. He was bone tired. His bones were too tired to dance. It didn't matter; he hadn't the time.

Inside Miloslav, right next to the love he had for the girl, something else began growing. And with each beat of his heart it grew larger and blacker. Like someone had left a pen uncapped, and it was all bleeding out. Bleeding out onto Miloslav's heart. A blackness, and a bleakness. Only trouble is, it was left on the wrong side. It blotted out his love for life, for himself, before it got even close to his love for the girl.

He started drinking after work the way people do to try and wash out the blackness. Only that wasn't enough. And so then he—

Miloslav slurped down the last of his forty and didn't say anything more for a while. I sat watching my shoes in the dirt.

"You what, Miloslav?" I asked.

"Othing," he said. "N-he-whey, is net e-noff."

"What's not enough," I asked.

All of it. Everything. Love, Miloslav said. *She kicked me out two weeks ago.*

"Oh," I said. I started peeling off the label of the forty. "That's too bad, man."

She'll take me back, Miloslav said, *she has to. It's love. She's—she`s taken me back before.*

Among the many things I wanted to say, I chose just this: "Man."

It'll work out.

I got up, frowning, and stretched. "I gotta get back to work," I said. I turned to Miloslav as he rose from the ground.

It was good seeing you, he said.

"You too," I said.

When he reached out his hand to shake mine, I saw the tiny pin-pricks, blackened and bruised, in the webbings of his paw.

"Take care, man," I said, shaking it.

Love isn't healthy for a bear, I should have said. Maybe it isn't healthy for any of us.

I saw Miloslav two months later. In the paper. He'd been arrested for possession of narcotics, paraphernalia, and causing a disturbance to the peace. I saw the article while I was at work. It featured this pathetic shot of Miloslav, bent over at the waist, being pushed inside the back of a cruiser by four officers in the middle of downtown.

"What is he?" one of my coworkers asked. The whole reason

something that small made it into the paper was that very question. What is he? What is Miloslav? The police were at that moment stumped, and Miloslav wasn't talking. Was in no condition to talk, from the looks of the picture.

"Maybe he got some kind of growth-hormone issue. Like Andre the Giant," another said.

"Whatever it is, they should put it down."

That there is the greatest dancer—the greatest artist—that ever lived, I wanted to say. But instead I took a bite of my sandwich.

After I finished eating, though, Miloslav ate at me. The picture in the paper. Him on the corner. Those tiny pinpricks between his paws. God knows where else he had to have 'em if he'd already resorted to shooting up in his paws. Miloslav's beautiful dancing body shorn and pock-marked with the most toxic bite made by man, and what did I ever do to stop it?

Miloslav, mid-spin, getting pegged in the head with a balled-up loaf of moldy bread.

What had I ever done to stop anything?

What was I? What kind of human? What kind of animal?

In between deliveries, I stopped at the bank and took out all I'd managed to save. A little over a thousand bucks. Part of me, the part that's like you and everyone else in this scum-loving, truth-sucking world, wanted to kick myself in the throat. But the other part of me, the part that stood in the back, palms slicking the broom in my hands with sweat as I watched Miloslav dance, understood. Miloslav was the closest thing to a friend I'd ever had. And if that didn't mean something, well then, nothing did.

The bondsman left me with thirty-five bucks. Enough to buy me and Miloslav some grub and a beer once I bailed him out of jail.

Miloslav stayed with me the next two weeks. When I'd leave for work, he'd be lying in a heap by my bedroom wall. When I came back, he'd be in that same heap. My own bear skin rug. His hair was growing back, slowly but surely, so everywhere along his body he was covered in this fine bristle. I laid a hand on the back of his neck once to check and see if he was still breathing, and the sharp hairs tickled and stung my palm.

Miloslav's hair had never been especially soft. It had never been especially clean, either. But it had never hurt to touch.

Try as I might, I couldn't get him to take off that stupid suit.

And try as I might, I couldn't get him to say much about the arrest.

I saw her getting dinner, he said.

"So?" I asked.

With someone else.

"Oh," I said.

Then the papers showed up informing him of the restraining order. I think he was clean before that. It was hard to tell. He told me he was clean before that. I believed he was clean, before.

I came home and there was music playing. I came home, and the whole apartment was shaking. I came home, and Miloslav had torn off his suit to lie in a heap on my bed. I came home and Miloslav was gone. In the middle of the floor were the papers. On them the address that he was to stay away from.

I figured that was probably where Miloslav was headed.

All the time I had spent with Miloslav must have rubbed off on me. I'd become dumb, and stubborn, and caring like some big, oafish animal. Like some strange dancer, swaying alone with their arms open.

Because I headed there, too.

Miloslav was in the yard when I got there, arms above his head, bellowing. I pulled up and laid on the horn and he turned his head for just a moment before turning back to the house. He let loose another bellow, a sour mix of an animal in pain and an angry man. A pale face appeared in the window, and then another behind it. The window slid open a few inches.

"Miloslav, stop," she said.

"We're calling the cops in a minute," a man shouted down.

Miloslav turned towards my car and for a moment I thought he was going to come. I thought he was finally going to walk away from all this unnatural love. To return. To the circus? To dancing? To the forest? To me? I wasn't sure. But he was going to escape, and that was what mattered most.

He popped the door open and I was hit by the smell of beer, rank and heavy. By the unnatural droop of his eye lids and the way they fluttered. He shouldn't even have even been able to stand.

"Urn ah rha-dee-o hup," he said.

"What?"

"Urn ah rha-dee-o hup. ehht, ehht, shex. Hai wh-an ou dans," Miloslav said.

"Miloslav, no."

"Rease,"

Behind him the two pale faces were still watching between the curtains, waiting to see if he'd leave.

MILOSLAV

"They're going to have you arrested and I've got no money to bail you out this time," I said.

Please.

Miloslav danced. I can't tell you what all too. Instrumentals, classics, they were never my strong suit. They never even came close to my closet, to be honest. But you know all about that from those nights I sat there twitching every time you put on one of your father's old albums and I'd fidget so bad I'd nearly come out my own skin. What I can say is sometimes the music was fast, and high, and jumping around like a frog or a honey bee in the Spring, and sometimes it was low, and heavy, and felt like rain at a funeral. No matter what, Miloslav danced. Even to the commercials. And no matter what he danced to, no matter with what speed he moved, there was an ache in every swing, every spin, every dip, every toss of his head. And there was love. So god-damn much of it I could barely breathe or move or think. It came at me like a wave and pulled me under to the deep, dark parts of the soul where all the terrifying, prehistoric things live alongside the last mysteries of our Earth.

Like what is Miloslav?

What does it mean to be human?

Why do we love? When love is such a cruel thing?

The faces between the curtains drew back eventually, and the curtains closed, but I had hardly noticed. I was already swept up in the under-toe by that point. And how couldn't you be? You'd have to be inhuman.

Miloslav danced for hours in the middle of suburbia, among the mowed lawns and the hip-high fences. A shorn bear in a shorn world, naked and rippling. The inky blue of the dawn was eaten away by the sun. People stepped out of their doors, keys in hands, and stopped to look at Miloslav for a moment, then turned their faces away and hurried to their cars, to their desk jobs, and away from their perfect houses and their loveless homes. Ashamed. Inhuman.

And Miloslav danced on.

And I sat, re-starting the car, idling the car, playing the music. Watching, as I always did, with wet eyes and my tongue pushed against the roof of my mouth. With something like a caged bird beating in my chest.

Until Miloslav fell.

And then I climbed out.

Miloslav had been unexpectedly light, when I dragged him back into my car. How is it a bear could be so light? Another mystery at the bottom of the ocean. Another mystery lost along with Milslov's swaying body, swinging legs. I stuffed him in the passenger seat and he slumped back, eyelids lopsided and fluttering, spittle oozing down his bristled jaw.

"You can't keep giving so much of yourself to people," I dug my fingernails into the steering wheel and leaned forward, as if that could get us further away faster from that woman, from that house. As if leaning forward could somehow suck the poison out of Miloslav's veins.

"Hwat 'ulse yam Hai sup-ou-sed ou Oo?" Miloslav asked.

"What?" I snapped, slamming on the brakes to look at him.

It took a moment for him to shake his face into a clear enough state to speak to me.

What else am I supposed to do?

"Keep something," I said. "Keep something for yourself."

I don't have anything but love. And love is something you have to give to others to have at all.

"You have your art," I said. "Goddammit, Miloslav, your art."

I was angry. I didn't like crying. I liked less people—even bears—seeing me crying. Maybe you don't believe that but that was how I was, before you. Before Miloslav.

Love. Art. It's the same thing. You have to give it. They're the same thing. Different names.

"Goddammit," I said again, and hit the gas. That would be the last thing I said to Miloslav. Goddammit.

He was asleep by the time we got to my apartment. And I was so tired. So very tired. Watching Miloslav dance. Seeing him empty himself like that. And all for what? For a very cruel thing: love. Something inside of me had snapped. And whatever it had been keeping closed had opened. And whatever had come out was too much. Too much for me, then. Too much for me now. I'm wasting here, see? Wasting away. It's all been too much. And it has been from the start. So I left him there to sleep it off in the car. Left him slouched over in the passenger seat, the greatest artist, man or animal, to ride out his high alone. And I went upstairs, and I fell face forward into my bed, then curled in. Curled in to try and tuck whatever had gotten loose in me back where it belonged. But it was too late. It was out.

And by the time I woke up and went out to my car. Miloslav was where I left him, in the passenger seat, slumped forward, a bib of crusted vomit laying over his stilled chest.

Miloslav was dead.

Dead. Stupid and dead.

And I want to blame him so bad for that.

Then, of course, I met you, and all that's happened here has happened. And I'd let it keep happening, you know. I'd keep right on doing the dance. Because it's in me, now. Moving freely. Tearing me apart. Beating away. Asking *please*. And isn't that what makes us human? Whatever this is inside me? Whatever made Miloslav dance for that girl in all the ways he danced. Love that girl in all the ways he loved.

But it's not in you, is it? It's me alone, left this way.

And I want to blame Miloslav so bad for that, too.

Anatomist

After the earthquake, she goes out collecting bones. It's easy enough. The ground of the graveyard has been split open, caving in near the center in a deep pit, from which several fissures run off in all directions. Like how a child draws a star. Or maybe like an asterisk. One to be tacked onto the sentence Rest in Peace*. (*Unless the dirt decides maybe it's too good for you one day, and spits you back up.) All around the crags, the ground is littered with bits of coffins, femurs, collarbones, and jaws. Teeth clustered like cigarette butts outside bars. She pockets these and can hear them rattle when she walks. Every now and then she slips a hand in and runs them through her fingers. The rest she gathers on a blanket and rolls up to carry fireman-style over her shoulder. She can only carry so many at a time, but she doesn't mind. It's good to get out of the house. It's good to have a hobby. Her tapes say so.

She steps too close to the edge of the pit and looks down. It goes deep. Deep-deep. So deep the darkness seems to take on mass. The dark looks solid enough to crawl out of the hole. To maybe say something. To maybe speak her name.

"Hello?" she says, and her voice bounces off its dirt walls before being muffled into nothing. She waits a moment, bent at the waist with an ear cocked towards the pit, but it doesn't reply. She sucks all her saliva to the back of her throat and hawks a loogie into it.

The boy hated stuff like that. Like when she had tried to spit into the mouth of a bass in a river below. Gross, he called it.

She feels embarrassed but misconstrues it for pride.

"It's rude not to respond," she tells the pit. She gathers her bones in her arms and picks her way between the fissures, out of the graveyard.

The FEMA man said that the building she lives in is mostly undamaged. That's subjective, she thinks. Part of the earth underneath the foundation crumbled so it sits at a slant. The same goes for the identical apartment building next to it. They've slumped together, their roofs resting against each other's like twin sisters dozing off in the back of a car. She had always wanted a twin. She thought a twin would come with a built-in permanent bond, and maybe telepathic powers. She may have thought the snuggling apartments were cute in their sleepy togetherness. She may have envied them. But it put her floor at such an angle that she couldn't keep anything still without nailing boards down for her furniture to catch on, so instead she's mostly just annoyed.

The FEMA man had told her about the boards and showed her how to set them up by doing it for her coffee table. He left her a few nails, a hammer because she didn't have one, and some wood. Like the rest of her things, they had slid against the wall in a heap.

That was all they could do for now, the FEMA man said. There was greater need all throughout the city. After things like this, hurt becomes quantifiable. Not all hurts are equal, or deserving of attention.

She and the graveyard remain distressed.

Although, to be honest, things aren't that different from before. She was never great at housekeeping. Only now her clutter is all in one place, and there are three near-complete skeletons on her couch.

Her front window is also broken, but she'd done that before the earthquake.

When she comes in, she lays the blanket across the skeletons' legs. Only the middle one has both, and it's in want of a foot and an arm. Every time she comes home they tell her what they're in need off.

"Did you bring me a clavicle?" says the one.

"A tibia?" says the second.

"If I had fingers, I could play the most beautiful melodies for you. Just get me a piano, and some phalanges." says the one again.

She has heard such promises before. The third one, her newest, doesn't say anything. He doesn't have the mandibles. He just stares at her with his sockets like the pit. But she knows this isn't his fault.

She loots her phone out of the clutter against the wall and checks it, but there's nothing from anyone she knows. Just strangers on apps trying to reach out to other strangers. Mostly for nudes, she thinks. She sets it back down, and it slides into the clutter. She lets it go. Don't let technology rule you. That's what one of her tapes said.

Next, she searches out her player, the one she bought from a thrift store before the quake, a book on anatomy she found in the ruins of the library, and her box of tapes. The last is the easiest to find. She always tucks it under the cushions of her couch. Sometimes it shifts around if the skeletons have squirmed while she is gone. But they never do that much. Back before the quake, and back before the broken window, when the boy used to lay with her on the couch, the tapes used to move a lot more. Sometimes the box would even open and all the tapes would spill out and she'd have to fish them out of the bottom of the couch one by one.

Always count things that could be worse, or once were worse, or even just different. Count what you can. Keep track of the quantities of your life. Run a tally.

That came from a tape, and the tapes had come from the old man upstairs, who liked to record himself reading self-help books. He left them outside his neighbor's doors. She kept them. She'd seen him looting through the dumpster and retrieving the ones chucked away. She felt sorry for him. And she also thought she could use some guidance. Now, they're the last two left in the building. Everyone else had somewhere else to go.

She has twenty-two tapes in total. She's never spoken to the man, but she knows his voice better than she knows her own father's, possibly even better than she knows her own. It's a road-rash voice. One that gets stuck in the ear and stays there. Every now and then it floats through her mind when she's out doing other things. She prefers this to when the boy's voice creeps in. His is only ever critical.

It was the old man's voice that had given her the idea about the bones. She had been walking past the graveyard on her way to where FEMA had set up its headquarters. The man with the boards had told her to register her name as a survivor down there, and that's what she was going to do. She wasn't, she told herself, going to check for the boy's name. She was just going to announce to the world that she was still here. Though no one yet had called asking. She'd gotten one message from a woman she didn't know yet, asking if she was alive. They were supposed to have coffee later that month. She didn't reply.

Care makes us human, the old man's voice told her. *Care is the cornerstone of civilization. Without it, we degrade into wildness. Without it, we dissolve into nothing. Care is what makes us real.*

All around, the houses were split in twos or threes or crumbled into nothing, fissures of broken concrete and grass stretching to their porches and reaching down into their foundations to shake them apart. Like tentacles from some Sci-Fi flick. The whole city had gone Lovecraft. Not even suburbia had survived. Fences and pink flamingos were tossed aside or swallowed. Across the road, the brick and wrought iron fence that had caged in the graveyard had crumbled and twisted like used tissue. A skull had bounced all the way out of bounds and onto the sidewalk. And did she care? Was she cared for?

We must find people who care. We must make people care. To make us real. Or else, we're nothing.

She knew *make* wasn't meant literally, but she also didn't see why it couldn't be. It seemed simpler than the alternative. Easier, in the long run. And so instead of going down to register as a survivor, she climbed the rubble of the fence into the graveyard.

That advice had come from a tape titled *Becoming a Real Person*, the most recent tape the old man had given to her. It's the one in her tape deck now, and so far she thinks it's the best out of all of them. Before this, her favorite had been *How to Keep Your Face Still When You Need To*. She'd listened to that one often back before the quake, when she had a job to go to and there were people in the streets. But now it isn't so important. She lets her face do what it wants.

She hits play and it starts mid-sentence:

"—without others' hands and eyes. How can you know you are flesh if there is no one there to touch you? To verify that this skin is here. This body is here. How can you be sure you can be seen, if there are no eyes to see you?"

She opens up the blanket and starts detangling the bones. The skeletons lean their heads forward to see what she's brought home.

"Have you ever wondered if these are real books?" asks the second skeleton.

She doesn't say anything back. She picks up a skull and runs her hands over it to brush the dirt off. Then she opens the anatomy book to the page about heads, necks, and shoulders.

"No," groans the first. "You promised you wouldn't start another."

The jawless skeleton's head rattles side to side to side until she reaches up and touches his empty knee socket.

"I'll see what I have for all of you," she says. "But look at this poor guy. His need is so great. He's got nothing." She holds the skull up so they can see into its eyes, and they quiet down.

Really, she knows once she gives them everything they need, only one of two things can happen. Either they'll leave. Or they'll want something more. Maybe their real teeth. Their real bones. Their real selves. Their real families. Things she can't give them. Which will just boil down to them leaving as well, but after giving her much more of a headache.

She doesn't need the tapes to tell her that.

"You will never be a real person until someone tells you you are a real person. Until then, you are nothing more than dust motes. You are nothing more than an accidental cluster of atoms. A photograph only partially developed."

She pulls a bone out of the pile and looks from it to the book. She never studied anatomy. Her two years in college had been wasted on pursuing a degree in fine arts with a focus on pottery. Back then she studied bodies in a casual, romantic way, but she'd never really known any of them for long. The only body she had ever really known was her own, and can one really accurately know one's body? And then she knew the boy's body, for a while. She knew the curve of his ribs, the bend of his elbow, the click of his jaw. She became a specialist in his anatomy. She knew when his spine curved a certain way and his fingers spread, she was becoming his world. She knew when his teeth clenched and shoulders hunched, bad weather was rolling in. She could still conjure pictures of his body behind her eyes.

She sets the skull between the knees of one of the skeletons. "Hold him still," she says. She gathers what looks to be scattered bits of spine. They aren't exactly the same size, but they will do. She uncaps her glue and turns to the skull.

The tape finishes, and she flips it and starts it again. The first skeleton groans, but the others stay quiet. She takes a break every now and then to check her phone. Sometimes she pulls up the news. There're warnings about aftershocks. The list of survivors has been published without her. She doesn't look. There's footage of buildings downtown collapsing in on themselves as the camera filming it shakes. There's footage of people crying. People sitting on the ground, dazed and dirt spackled, under long pavilion styled tents. There is a moment where she catches sight of a survivor and nearly recognizes him as him. It's hard to know for sure, because it's only someone in the background. It's only someone who is covered in dust and moving with purpose towards someone else, their face only partially caught by the camera. It is only just a glimpse, and whenever she catches glimpses of someone who looks enough like him, she is always recognizing them as him. It means nothing.

She rewinds it anyway to watch one more time. And then again.

"He's dry now," the one calls from the couch.

She sets her phone down and it slides back into the clutter. The newest skeleton is just a spine, shoulder blades, and an arm. She'll bring him ribs if she can find them tomorrow. Tomorrow, he'll be awake. For now, she props him up against the end of the couch so his arm dangles over the armrest.

She works on the others, filling in their gaps. She gives the third the rest of an arm, a piece of pelvis, finishes one of his legs down to his foot. The first gets all the fingers. The second gets a foot and some toes. She works until after midnight and all that's left in the blanket are bits of bone shard so fine they look like sugar.

She stands up and wraps the blanket around herself like a cape and then drops down between the third skeleton and the newest one. The third skeleton turns his face towards her, his skull bouncing on the base of his spine. She reaches up to touch his cheekbone.

"Tomorrow I'll find you a jaw," she promises.

She wakes to a thump on her door sometime past ten. She untangles herself from the blanket and the bones. The morning is always the worst. Dew slips in the broken window and soaks the clutter against the wall and the top of the couch. It even gets in her hair and wets the top of the skeletons' skulls. Their teeth rattle in their sleep from the cold. But there isn't enough space in her bed for all of them. It's also the hardest to fight against the tilt of her floor in the mornings. She keeps forgetting the shape of the world in her sleep, and the first steps of the day are always surprising.

At the door, lying on her mat, is a tape. The front door of her building is hanging open and outside she hears a car door slam. Voices bickering. She steps out into the hall and looks out. At the curb there's a station wagon idling, and a man and woman talking over the roof. In the backseat the old man from upstairs sits. In the hatch are a few suitcases and filled trash bags. The woman lowers herself into the car, and the man looks back once at the apartment building. He sees her standing there, and gives her a strained smile before dropping into the car as well.

The old man doesn't look at all before the car pulls off.

She walks out the door and stands at the curb. She can still smell the smog from their exhaust pipe. She looks down the road and watches as the car rocks over a makeshift bridge of boards stretched over a fissure in the ground. She wants to stand there and watch them until they're out of sight, but with the road the way it is, it's slow going. The fact that they made it at all is surprising. It`s evidence of great care.

She feels grief and misconstrues it as anger.

She turns around and walks back into her apartment, leaving the tape on the mat.

"Are you going to the graveyard?" the one asks, but she walks past them and closes herself up in the bathroom. She sits on the toilet and hangs her head between her knees and counts her toes.

Without another person to witness your life, does your life mean anything at all?

It's too much for me to handle on my own, the boy says. *I can't be the one to take care of you.*

She closes her eyes and can see the haze of station wagon exhaust. The old man's face smeared behind tinted glass. The woman and the man sitting together upfront, having a small argument.

She feels jealousy and misconstrues it as betrayal.

She lets herself sit with that misunderstanding until she dozes off.

There is a scratching at the bathroom door. She wakes to it. She thinks about letting it be, but as if the sound can read her mind, it grows more frantic. She thinks of gouges in the wood. She wonders if her landlord is dead.

When she opens the door, it's her favorite, the third, laying outside. His arm is outstretched and the hand is still flapping up and down on his wrist. He stares up at her.

She gathers him up in her arms and carries him back to the couch.

"You can't let us keep living like this," says the second. "Being incomplete is torture."

The fourth is still asleep. She can see pearls of glue that have oozed out between the seams of his spine. When he wakes, will he wake disoriented? That's how it was with the others. All of them came to screaming. Except for the third. She had seen to that when she cracked his jaw off in the cemetery.

She feels empathy but misconstrues it as pity.

"Okay," she says. "Fine."

She takes three shopping carts from the ruined dollar store down the road. She'll need some kind of rope to be as efficient as possible, and she'll need more glue from inside. The store caved in completely. Its roof lays on top of its remains like a stone tablet cracked in two. She has to pull out stone after stone before she can squeeze under it and crawl through the remains of the store's guts.

When she's inside, there's only just enough light to make out the vague shape of things in the dark. Bits of plastic toys dig into the palms of her hands. She feels her way through puddles of water and soda. Feels wet stuffing between her fingers. She remembers a story she was told as a child. About a stuffed rabbit that wanted to be made real. *Care is key*.

The old man should not have acted like he was lonely if he was not alone.

She presses forward, feeling her way through the half-light. She hits a wall of rubble. Follows it to the right, and her hand lands in something wet again. When she reaches forward she feels soft flesh and the edge of cloth. She stares down at where she knows her hand to be until the darkness takes the shape of an arm sprouting out of a polo shirt. A torso with a name tag she can't read.

She wonders for the first time what she'll do when the world rights itself. When the people who can go back to living finally do go back to living. The world will shake off the dust and march on, and those who can't march along will go back in the dirt. They'll dissolve into phantoms.

She holds the hand of the corpse. She feels fear and misconstrues it as grief.

The building shakes. Beneath her the earth bucks. She lets go of the corpse's hand and curls into a ball. The aftershock passes.

"Sorry," she says, and crawls over the body. She keeps crawling, and keeps searching until her hands brush against yarn, soft and unspooled and just strong enough to handle what she needs of it.

She pulls the train of carts she tied together into the graveyard. She is covered head to toe in dollar store dust. It's in her eyes, causing the light to sparkle and pop like there are fairies floating all around her. It's in her mouth, making everything taste like plaster and mold. It is on her skin, dying her white as a plastic bag. She feels closer to the bones than ever before.

She begins to load the carts, picking bones indiscriminately. Her choices have always been uneducated, but she had looked, at least, before. Tried to imagine which parts might fit where. Now she just brings arm loads to the shopping carts and dumps them in, one after the other. When her arms are empty she runs through the graveyard till they're full again. Already, the sun is setting. She'd been under the rubble for longer than she thought.

She comes to the mouth of the pit when all but the last cart are completely full, and she looks down into it. The black of it is seeping up. Reaching out towards her.

There is a nothing inside of all of us. We are nothing, all of us. We need others to act as mirrors. So that we can be vigilante against the parts of ourselves that would eat the rest of us whole, says the old man.

The way you act is irrational, says the boy.

I never know who I'm talking to.

I think I've never really known you at all.

She kicks her foot into the dirt and a clump of it comes loose and falls into the pit, cartwheeling as it goes. It slips from view. She imagines running behind the carts until they pick up enough speed, then jumping on the back. She imagines them all plummeting over the edge and falling together.

"If you have something to say then say it," she says. But the pit just throbs, and the sun goes down.

She props the door to her building open and pushes the carts up the slanted floor towards her door. When she gets there the tape is gone and the door is ajar. Inside she can hear the old man's voice. She releases the carts and they roll back to hit her in the stomach. She buckles for a moment before moving out of the way. The carts roll past her and smash into the wall, scattering bones all over the floor. She ignores this in favor of the door.

Someone, she thinks, has come back. Maybe the old man. Or maybe someone's come to see if she's alive. Maybe someone she used to work with. Or maybe even her family. Or maybe even the boy.

As she opens the door, she can see him, shoulders hunched over the player in the dark of her apartment. The old man's voice, the new tape, is playing.

"When I was a boy I used to think about colors. How we saw them. How we could never be sure that what we were seeing was like anyone else was seeing. We look at something and call it blue, but how can I know that my blue is your blue?"

She steps closer and rubs dollar store out of her eye. "Honey?" she asks, and he turns his head. But there are no eyes. No nose. No body.

"Are you the one who brought me here?" asks the fourth skeleton.

"How can we know that our reality matches anyone else's? Language is a trap. It falls short of any true meaning. It is a fool's comfort. And feelings? We learn the names of our feelings because people tell us what we are feeling when we are feeling it based on what they can see. But how can they truly know what we're feeling? So then, how can we?"

The three are asleep on the couch. Except maybe the third. She can never tell with the third. Is he watching her? Did he let the fourth touch her things? Did he let him open the door? Did he let him fool her into thinking that there was someone coming for her?

The fourth pushes and pulls himself away from the player towards her. He reaches for her ankle, and she backs away.

"You have to finish me up," he says. "I can't stand being this way."

She feels pity but misconstrues it as revulsion. She kicks his hand away and he rolls down the floor and clatters against the wall.

"I wanted to share with you what I felt and what I saw, but there's no true way."

She seizes the skeleton out of the clutter and hoists him up against the wall. She pounds him against it, over and over. He screams. She screams Bits of bone splinter. Spine falls to the floor.

"I'm a failure when it comes to being a person. Maybe we all are. I'm sorry."

Something hard comes down across the top of her skull and her vision becomes all bright bursts of color. She drops the skeleton and they fall together to the floor. She catches sight of the third skeleton, her favorite. His eye sockets are so very close to hers. Then all she can see is nothing.

She wakes to the sound of rattling bones and music. She can't stand up. Her body is bound with unwound tapes. From the floor, all she can see is ankle bones, spinning and stomping and sliding down the angled floor in pairs to stomp back up it together. She rolls onto her back and tries to prop her head up to get a better view, but before she can, hands grip her ankles and drag her across the floor. Then hands are all over her. She wants to scream but there is tape ribbon lodged in her mouth and around her tongue.

The hands hoist her up and hold her steady. In her apartment, there are wall-to-wall skeletons, dancing. In the corner the one stands, playing the piano, while another bangs on her pots and pans. She tries to count how many and loses track. There are more in the hall. They begin to pour in, and the music grows louder. They form a circle. They spin her around and around and pass her to the next in line. The tape gets caught under her feet sometimes, and she nearly falls, but the next set of hands catches her, lifts her back up, and sets her spinning again.

When she comes full circle, they shove her backwards into the middle. She is sure she is falling when she feels hands hook under her shoulders and drag her back up. She's turned around once more. Her favorite is holding her, very nearly complete, but still jawless.

He takes the tape ribbon from out of her mouth and unwinds her slowly. A skeleton steps forward with a jaw and a bottle of glue. Her favorite takes them once she is untied. He holds them out to her.

Once something is finished, it's finished, the boy says. All around her are empty eyes. The music has stopped.

Her favorite presses the jaw into her hand. She can feel the teeth press into her palm. Behind her there is a wall of ribs. She closes her eyes and closes her fingers around the bone. She reaches up to his face and his hands guide her hands to the empty seam.

There is a great cheer, and the music starts up again. When she opens her eyes, they're all filing out of her apartment, new limbs flailing. The third stands before her, wiggling his jaw. He lays a hand on her shoulder and says something, but she can't hear him over the music. Two skeletons pick up the piano and carry it so the first can keep playing as he walks. The apartment empties. She can hear them in the street through the shattered glass of her window.

Before the last few are gone the third hoists her up and carries her out the door after them.

They whirl together down the street. Sometimes they do the foxtrot. Sometimes it's the tango. Sometimes he sends her spinning and she freewheels through the skeletons, crashing into them and nearly falling. She's never sure if it's him that takes her hand again, but it no longer seems important. She catches sight of another parade making their way out of downtown. Trucks branded with FEMA drive slowly up the wreckage of the main road. People trail behind, backpacks slung over their shoulders, or jumbled possessions clutched in their arms. For a moment, she thinks they're going to merge, but the skeletons veer away. They're heading into the cemetery. She pulls away from the skeletons and watches the survivor procession as it draws closer. The trucks stop in the road when they see the skeletons. The survivors on foot draw alongside them.

Hands spider around her hips and she feels a collarbone press into the back of her neck. Someone lifts her, and she allows herself to be lifted. She's hoisted upwards, spread out on her back over the hands of a cluster of skeletons, as if she were crowd surfing through them. Up ahead, the leaders have made it to the edge of the pit. She watches the white caps of their head drop down and disappear only to be followed by the next. It looks like a river churning over the brink of a waterfall. The piano goes, and the player after it. The sounds of pots and pans banging is replaced by the quiet murmur of grass under feet and the hum of idling trucks.

She tilts her head back towards the survivors. Everyone looks the same, upside down and far away. Or maybe, everyone looks the same when your heart is hurt and hopeful.

They all look like him.

The earth shakes again and she feels the bones of the many hands holding her shake as well. She looks back and sees the pit widening, clumps of dirt loosening and tumbling under the feet of the skeletons, who follow the earth down into the dark. Still, the ones carrying her surge forward to the opening mouth of it, and she rides along.

All I ever wanted was to be known by someone. To feel one with others, the old man says.

The hands around her ankles let go as the skeletons holding them drop downward. She sits up to look one last time at the survivors. Is one stepping forward? she thinks, but before she can tell, the skeletons beneath her knees and thighs are gone, and it's too late. She turns to the pit and stares down its dark eye. Then she reaches out her arms and leans forward.

She hears her name being called.

The Way of the Dinosaurs

This is the way the world ends:

We're sitting in a hole in the wall bar down on Lincoln, and it's noon or a little after on a weekday. But it's packed. Nobody is at work. People stopped going last Tuesday when the meteor was finally deemed unavoidable. Or maybe Earth was deemed unavoidable since the meteor is the one moving and all. We're crammed in at the counter, watching the meteor on a small TV that's only really fit for unimportant things like sports and music videos. The meteor looks so small that I feel like I could simply pluck it out of the sky and put it in my back pocket to save for later.

"This is the way the world ends," you say again.

I chew my straw and watch you look around the bar at all the other doomed faces staring up at the monitor like turkeys in a rainstorm.

"With one last happy hour," I say, spitting the straw out of my mouth. But you don't smile so I try something else. "Isn't that from a poem?"

You turn your attention to your phone, but there's nothing going on there that hasn't been going on all week. Goodbyes from your mom, from your friends. I turned mine off after the third day.

I was exhausted by farewells. I only wanted them from you.

"Waiting for a word from some sweetheart I don't know about?" I ask. Your mouth bends like a bow, but you don't answer. The footage cuts to other cities. Other countries. All over there are moving scenes—mother's holding their children one last time and weeping, strangers swaying and singing together at candlelight vigils for the entire human race, lovers holding impromptu weddings in the street. Whoever has taken it upon themselves to man the camera avoids the ugly. The bodies of the suicides. The looting. The spats of violence I've seen break out with my own eyes but did nothing to stop. As if in these final moments, we could rewrite the history of the world. Make man something sweeter, softer, kinder. I want to thank them, whoever they are. I am open to revision.

"We should do that," I say, motioning to the screen as a woman in a tux lifts a veiled woman off the street. They try to kiss even while they're still laughing.

"Don't be ridiculous," you say, tapping your phone and snapping your eyes around the bar again.

"I'm not." I stand up and reach across the counter to grab a bottle of rum. "One last drink for the road, darling?" I say, like I've said for the last five or six glasses. By the time I'm done pouring, you're crying.

"I thought," you start, then bite your lip the way you do when you think you're about to say something I won't understand.

"Thought we'd have more time? Have a family? Grow old together?"

"I thought at least my death would be mine. No one else's. That it'd be special." You slip your phone off the counter and into your pocket. I slide my stool closer and bump your knees with my own.

"It is special. We get to all go together. We get to share it with everyone. It's kind of Buddhist, right?" I smile and reach for your hand, but you move it to wipe your face.

"You don't know anything about Buddhism," you say. "This has nothing to do with Buddhism."

I turn back to my drink and stir it with my chewed straw. The ice melted but I don't bother getting more. I'm working up to it. To saying something I need to. I'm about to say everything. All the things you've ever wanted to hear and more.

You slip off your stool, running the heel of your palm against your eyes. "I can't do this. Not like this." You turn into the crowd.

"Are you leaving me? Now?" I ask, but the space where your body was has already filled. All around me a wall of people closes in. You've already left.

I turn back to the TV and the meteor is on screen again. Hurtling. Hurtling. Hurtling.

"Just like the dinosaurs, eh?" The man next to me mumbles. "Everything we've done will count for shit now."

"I wonder what'll come next?"

"Imagine them finding our bones."

I close my eyes and picture us as we were when we were younger. In the fall when we used to hike in the mountains. I picture us on a summit. I'm lifting you the way I used to when you saw the perfect red leaf just about to fall from its branch that you couldn't wait to have. The meteor is coming. It's headed straight to your open arms, and we're both smiling. This is how they'll find our bones, I say. It won't be in some bar. It won't be alone. I breathe in the fresh mountain air and hear your singsong sigh.

"This is the way the world ends."

Just as the earth begins to shake.

This is Where You Leave Me

The train station at the end of the world sits on a cliff above the great expanse. The road to it takes you around a mountain of layered rock twisted into a shape not unlike a tightened rosebud. The station is perched on the lip of one of the petal outcroppings, and the track trails off it down into the milky nothing like a snapped spider web. The stone of the mountain is a pale, sand-dune brown, almost pink in the dawn's light. The train station is a tin shack about as tall and broad as a farmhouse, and as long as an airplane hanger. Its tail end hangs off the lip of the ledge above the nothing. The building is dappled with rust that eats clean through it in some patches. There's one lone conductor that stands at the top of the stairs.

There is only one platform. There's only one train. It goes only one way.

I had a friend that went there before all this. In return, I got a postcard of the station with their name typed on the back at the bottom.

Lousy going away present. Lousy farewell. Then again, they always are.

<3

In August, the nights are always dark and violent with the death of the season. I hated those times; transitional times. They were always hard on me. It was in August that I kissed you on the mouth outside of a bar.

The bar's insides had been just as dark as the night, and though I'd stood next to you while the band played and bodies milled around, and had even held your hand, I had yet to see your face clearly. I liked you by smell. It was a clean-sheet smell, with the tang of a nervous sheen of sweat underneath.

I followed you outside and lit a cigarette and smoked at your back.

"Nice band," I said.

"Yeah," you said.

"You seem nice," I said.

"Thanks," you said.

"These things have been really hard for me," I said.

"They can be," you said.

"I just used to come here with a friend of mine," I said. "But they're gone now."

You turned and put a hand on my shoulder and I leaned into you.

"We've all got missing stuff," you said. "I'm sorry."

I leaned my head back and our lips touched, then parted, and then pressed into each other harder. When I came away, there was something warm and small and round on my tongue. I pulled it out between my fingers. A pale, pink light sputtered between us.

That was the night I spit out the glow worm. And I saw you come into focus.

<3

After my friend had gone, I had looked into the train station. On the internet I read stories about it. About the famous musician who went up the mountain and came back, his head shaved and a thick seam running down the arc of his head. How he never wrote another song after that and never appeared in public.

A man followed his wife up once, but the conductor wouldn't let him on the platform. He had to watch from the bottom of the stairs as she boarded, as she stood stone-faced in the frame of the last car's window, and as the train coughed itself alive.

I had stories like this printed and left out all over my desk, and the postcard pinned to my wall. I bought paintings of the station. Books about it. Little keychains of the rosebud mountain and miniatures of the black steam engine. There were maps showing the way to it. I had a few. But try as I might I could never find any map of its routes, or timetables of when the train came. There were no tickets on sale, but I did find a bus schedule to the town at the foot of the mountain.

I packed everything away, the night of the glow worm, and set up a small aquarium for it in its place. I put everything about the station at the end of world into a chest and pushed it into the back of my closet.

The only thing the glow worm would eat was leaves coated in honey and a light dusting of sugar. At first, it was easy to feed, but it grew as time went on. From a pebble to the size of my pinky to the length of my palm. You used to come and sit by its aquarium with me at my desk and watch as it inched across the glass floor, shimmering. We'd take it out and shut the lights off and let it crawl back and forth across our linked hands.

"It's getting so big," you whispered, and pressed your lips to my cheek.

"I hope it lasts the winter," I said. "It gets cold."

"Can I help?" you asked.

"You should move in with me," I said. "You should help me take care of it."

"Really?" you asked.

"It's yours, too," I said.

The glow worm had looped its long body around and around our fingers. I could feel its tiny feet scratching against my palm, and I thought this is a good feeling. These are good things to think.

Not about snapped webs arcing above the mist, floating as if they were tetherless. But about growing things.

For the first three days of the New Year we were stuck inside thanks to a blizzard. By then, the glow worm was as fat as the desk its aquarium had once sat on. At night, we had to close the door to our bedroom so that its light wouldn't keep us awake.

"We save so much on electricity," I used to say as I wrapped my arms around you from behind and kissed your shoulder.

"We lose more in feeding it," you'd say back, leaning into me. We had to buy our sugar and honey in bulk and use spinach during the winter. At first it had been finicky about the change, but eventually it took. It had to.

During those three days the glow worm curled up under the desk and we ran a kerosene heater constantly. I had just quit smoking, and all I wanted to do was sleep, sleep, sleep, until the bugs that were marching through my veins and gnawing away at my brain had died off. We curled together on the bed, and I dozed off and on while the snow beat against the window in a constant wave. It was Heaven, I thought as my eyelids closed, coming down to Earth in one huge chunk to bury us all in bliss.

But I saw mist in my dreams instead.

I woke up to the sound of rummaging, and a gentle, persistent hiss. When I opened my eyes, you were half in the closet, and the chest was half out. Scattered around you were the papers I had printed.

"What are you doing?" I asked.

You emerged from the closet, the bus schedule in one hand, the postcard in the other.

"What is this?" You asked. "Why do you have them?"

"It's old," I said, "It's just old stuff."

You opened your mouth and held them out towards me but the hiss had risen to a tea-kettle screech.

"What is that?" I asked.

I rushed past you, past the postcard, past the bus ticket, and was hit with the stench of burning grass. The glow worm was thrashing against the kerosene heater; its skin soldered to the hot metal.

The first cigarette I had in three months and seventeen days was in March. Mid-way through the month. I'd kept track of it. Every day was a bloodstain on a calendar that would add up to a better life someday not yet reached. I had the next cigarette two days later. And then three more the week after. I stood outside and smoked them next to the dumpster, threw the rest of the pack in when I was done, then sprayed myself with deodorant every time I went back inside.

It was easy sneaking out then. The glow worm had grown to

half the size of the living room. We had to bring in whole trash bags full of leaves once a day and slather them with honey and a pound of sugar. The house always smelled a little like dirt and earth, so it was easy not to notice the smell of smoke. And there was so little space so suddenly, we were both happy whenever any spare bit was freed up. Absences weren't only forgiven, but encouraged.

When I finished the fifth cigarette of that year, I threw the rest away as I always did, with a grimace and a promise and a twinge like a needle pinching into my spine, and headed back in. You were in the kitchen with headphones on cooking dinner. On the floor, the desk lay overturned in a heap of bills, cups, and electronic devices on top of the glow worm.

"Hey," I said. I got nothing back.

"Hey," I said again, coming into the kitchen and shouting it loud enough so you could hear. You snapped your headphones off and looked at me startled.

"Can you come help me with this?" I said, gesturing towards the mess in the living room.

"I'm kind of busy."

"Jesus Christ, please," I said.

We hoisted the table up and threw everything back on top of it willy-nilly. You had to reach under the glow worm to retrieve your laptop. The screen was a shattered web of glass by the time you got it free.

"Fuck," you said. "Fuck."

You threw it across the room and it thudded against the wall.

"It's getting worse," you said, shoving the brittle brown end of the glow worm away from you. The burnt tissue from the heater had spread as quickly as the glow worm had grown. It stretched all the way from its tail end to halfway up its body.

"It's not," I said. "This isn't—it's not damage. It's not from that. Wounds don't get bigger as they heal."

"Maybe it's not healing," you said.

"Maybe it would if you'd just fucking help take care of it."

I went to the corner and pulled a bag of leaves out of the pile and began spreading it on the floor next to the glow worm's pulsing mouth. With each fistful of leaves I pulled out, I glared up at you. We'd trained it by then, to take it without the honey and sugar.

"Are you seriously going to cry?" you asked. "Seriously? It broke my laptop."

"It's yours, too," I said. "It needs care."

And then I was sobbing. Like I would on and off, all the time, since the first of the year.

"Jesus Christ, calm down." You took my shoulders in your hands. First rough. Then soft. And then you were cradling me. We eased down against the bag of leaves and I cried wet patches into your shirt.

"It's fine," you said. "I needed a new one anyway."

When I stopped crying, we sat up and looked at the laptop laying against the wall.

"I need my own space or something," you said after a while. I tensed, and if you felt it or not, I don't know, but you eased into me. "Like, maybe we could put a desk in the bedroom."

"There's no room with the dresser," I said.

You stood then and left me alone on top of the bag of leaves, and brushed yourself off while trying not to glare at me.

"There would be. We could put the dresser in the closet if you just got rid of all that stuff in that chest," you said. "Just keep the postcard. The rest is just—it's just trash."

"It means something," I said. "I can't just throw it away."

"Jesus Christ," you said, and you put your headphones back in and went to the kitchen.

The glow worm squirmed next to me, its mouth puckering, trying to reach a cluster of leaves on the ground just out of its reach.

I'd wake up in the middle of the night and sneak out to smoke. Too often I had to crouch under the open lid of the dumpster to try and avoid the summer thunderstorms as they rolled in, one after the other. Sometimes you knew I smoked, and you'd snort and turn from me and I'd tell you I'll try again, I'll try again, and sometimes then you would give my shoulder a squeeze and say I know you can do it.

When I'd come back in, I'd go to the chest. I'd take everything out and lay it on the floor as you slept. Every night everything seemed to be in a different spot then where I had placed it. I was afraid one night I'd come in and find something missing. Something that had some clue, or something that spoke some truth about what decides what leaves from the station at the end of the world, and why and where to. I didn't think you'd taken anything. I wasn't sure. I wanted to believe you wouldn't.

But it was hard for me to know what you were doing when you spent all your time in the bedroom with the door shut.

I tried to remember the exact location of where I put every single thing when I repacked it, but somehow I was left with only a vague sense of unease when I opened it back up. Like something delicate and forgotten had broken inside, but I could only hear the rattle of it shifting around.

After, I would go out to feed the glow worm. It had to be fed by hand since the crust that had grown around it had reached up to the very top. All that was open by mid-July was the mouth.

Not long after, that closed up too.

A week after it did, you pushed me to get rid of the leaves. I wasn't comfortable with the idea, but eventually I gave in. After we tossed the last bag, you stood staring at me, arms crossed over your chest.

"What do we do about it," you said, nodding to the glow worm.

"What do you mean?" I asked.

"We've got to get rid of it somehow. Do you want to bury it?"

"No, I don't want to bury it. Are you fucking nuts?"

"It's dead," you said.

"It's not dead." I climbed down on the floor and laid my hands against it. The crust—the scar—the shell or whatever it was, was hard, but flaky. Pineconish. It felt cool, despite the summer heat. Like a stone plucked from the bottom of a deep river. I put my ear to it and closed my eyes.

"I can hear its heart beating," I said. "Just come listen."

"You're delusional," you said.

"Just listen," I said, sitting up. "Is that hard for you to do? To listen? To care a little?"

You stared at me and I stared at you. Then I lowered myself back down to the ground and pressed my ear back against the glow worm.

I heard the bedroom door slam shut.

<3

I printed pictures of cocoons and slipped them under the bedroom door. It'd been so long since I'd seen your face during the day, I wasn't sure what it looked like anymore. I only came in the middle of the night, to check the chest. To look towards you in the dark.

"It's a cocoon," I called. "Come look at this. It'll open up someday."

I waited for a moment, with my ear against the door, and listened to you breathing slowly.

"It's just going to take some time," I said.

From beyond the door I heard the shuffle of the sheets and your footsteps, slow and hesitant. I closed my eyes and pressed my ear against the door.

"Wait," I said.

"That isn't what this is," you said.

"Just come out and look it over," I said.

A moment of silence passed, and then I felt something brush against my knee. When I looked down, I saw you had shoved the papers back under the door.

"Just open up," I said.

From further away, I heard your voice muffled by the pillows.

"It's dead," you said. "Why can't you see that it's dead."

"Just wait," I pleaded.

When you said nothing else, I took the pictures and crawled across the floor to the glow worm. I laid my head against it and tried to listen for the faint beat. Something, anything, that might convince you it wasn't over.

One night I stepped out to buy cigarettes, and as was my custom, I stood outside smoking them one after putrid other by the dumpster, shivering and gagging in the black, violent night of August. I could stand out there for an hour and a half, doing that. And I did, frequently.

When I came back inside, the glow worm was gone, and the bedroom door was open. I called your name as I went to the bedroom, and hoped for one blind foolish moment that you had come out, you had heard the heartbeat, and then you had decided to pull it with you into the bedroom. To cradle it in our blankets until it was ready to hatch.

But then I saw the chest overturned in the middle of the room. Everything had poured out across the floor. Everything but the bus schedule.

The town at the foot of the mountain was small but packed together densely in tall concrete buildings painted in pastels. Despite the empty streets and the cold, clinical taste to the air, it had an artificial warmth to it. As if the whole town were a smiling sticker slapped on a child's IV stand. I had looked at it time and time again. Cruised through it on digital maps. Or in books. Or paintings. Stepping off the bus felt like I was stepping out of consciousness into a dream without having fallen asleep. But it was an effect I didn't have time to appreciate. I ran through the narrow streets, following black arrows painted on buildings towards the start of the mountain. I kept running until the incline became too steep, and my breath was shooting out of me in short, sharp wheezes.

I'd caught the next bus, an hour after yours. You had a head start. But you also had the glow worm on your back.

Round the mountain I went, and round the mountain I went, and with each turn the town dropped further and further away, and on the other side of the cliff, the mist got thicker and thicker in the air. Each mouthful dissipated in my mouth and left the taste of rubbing alcohol and fresh mint; hospital clean and burning.

Sometimes I had to stop when I was free of it and just breathe, but almost every time I did, I'd picture the platform, empty save for a trail of smoke wafting out of over the tracks, and the conductor standing there with a new postcard in hand.

The spirals became tighter, until the mist hung around the mountain like garland, and I could barely see where I was placing my feet. How you could manage it with such a heavy load, I didn't know. You must be determined, I thought, and it stung as deep as the mist.

Then the walls burgeoned out again, and the path grew narrower when the petals pushed out, and only widened as they curved back in. It was slow going then, and I had to press myself to the wall to stay on the path. I began to worry that you could have dropped the glow worm. Or that you could have fallen.

By the time I came to the top, my clothes were soaked through with sweat and smelled of the mist. Across the stretch of sandstone, I saw you hauling the glow worm across the ground towards the stairs of the station. Despite the sore, clean ache in my lungs, I found the strength to run..

By the time I got within a shout's reach, you were already mounting the stairs. The conductor stepped forward and looked you over, and you stepped aside to show him the glow worm.

"Just dropping off," you said, your voice skipping across the stone expanse.

I tried to shout, but there was no wind in me. Instead, I sprawled forward and skidded against the ground, got to my feet and hobbled the rest of the way to the stairs.

"Stop," I managed to say at last, but you had already hoisted the top half of the glow worm back into your arms and were dragging it towards the last train car. I got to the first step, and the conductor grabbed me by the shoulder.

"Sorry," he said. "Passengers only."

"It's not dead." My voice was hoarse, raw, and weak, and you didn't even turn towards it. I looked towards the conductor, but he just held me by the shoulder and looked off in the distance. When I tried to push past him he twisted me around and held me by both my elbows so I couldn't do anything but watch as the door slid open.

"It's not dead," I said. "It's not."

You put the glow worm in the back cab and turned to walk towards us with your head down. When the doors had closed, the conductor eased his grip on my elbows.

"How could you do that?" I came towards you, quicker than I had meant, as if a burst of speed could make up for the time I lost before the end. You didn't look up. Your hands sprung out between us and you shoved me backwards.

"You need to learn to let go," you hissed between your teeth, and for one moment I saw your face turned towards me, before you were past me and running across the stone.

I looked back to the train and saw a light, pale and pink, throbbing in the final car. It grew, and then something velvety and thin brushed against the corner of the window.

"It's hatching," I screamed, turning around to watch you run. "Just come back! It's hatching." But you didn't turn to look until you were already so far away I couldn't make out your face when you did. And then you were going again.

The train whistled and a billow of smoke filled the station. When the smoke cleared, I watched as a flood of butterflies, glowing softly, fluttered up into the window's line of sight, filling the cabin, floating in the air, crawling against the glass.

And then, the train pulled away.

The Center of Everything

There is a being smack dab in the center of the universe. It sits at the very point from which everything imploded out, and to which one day everything will slowly return. We're nothing more than a dust mote in its eyes. A pore in its nipple. On top of its head are two large antlers, around which whole galaxies hang like sparkling garland from a tree. Its name is Asmoff.

I saw it in your eyes, the very first time I lost you.

Here's what love is; it's one giant gulp of air that you hold so long it hurts. But once you let it go, you feel empty. So achingly empty.

The first time we fall in love you are in your last year of college and I am already out, working a shit job, and hanging out with all the same people at all the same places I was when I was in school. We meet at one of those Halloween pub-crawls, and when we bump into each other we're unrecognizable to even ourselves. But there's something about the way you smell that speaks to me in a primal way. In the language of blood and butterflies.

By the time I finish trying to pat dry the beer I spilled on your shirt, and you lift your mask, I'm already in love. When I do catch a glimpse of your face it's all over for me. Not just for that lifetime, but for all others, too. For eternity.

You had the most beautiful birthmark below the corner of your mouth. Like you'd just spit out a miniature key. The kind used to open diaries or wind music boxes. That was the first place I kissed, just shy of your lips by two centimeters. It was the same place I'd kiss for the next three years, morning in, night out.

It's how much I talked about that birthmark that eventually annoyed Asmoff into making the bet.

Is Asmoff God? It is at the center of all things. It is, as far, as I can tell, the largest being in existence. It can manipulate matter in a way beyond human understanding, and understand things far beyond physical matter. Time is nothing to it. Death is nothing to it. Everything is nothing to it.

So maybe it is God. I don't know.

It's no romantic, that's for sure. And it's also kind of an asshole.

"You shouldn't be here," Asmoff told me when I first came face to face with it. One month before this, I had spotted it in your eye. It appeared there when your pupil relaxed with your last breath.

"Where is here?" I asked. I supposed I'd drunk myself straight into the grave, and I was more or less right.

Asmoff looked at me closer, cupping its hands around the nothingness I floated in and pulling me up to one of its eyes. Suddenly, it was my whole world, that eye. The murky-clear curve of it. Inside were churning clouds of dust and fog, coming together to form astral bodies for mere seconds before they'd blow apart into nothing but particles again. It was days I laid under that eye being scrutinized, watching planets form and unform.

"You," Asmoff finally said, pulling me back. "I saw you see me."

"You were there when he died," I said. "In his eye."

My heart was like a beehive thrust into a fire whenever I remembered that moment. All blind stinging and panic. It is still, despite the lives I've lived in between.

"Who?" Asmoff asked.

That was the first question Asmoff had ever asked another being. And it was a question it would come to regret. Not just in the next few days, but for centuries. For eons, even.

"My person," I began.

Here's what love is; It's sitting down at a poker table full of professional card counters with empty pockets and betting the rest of your future on a hand you don't get to see.

It's not that there weren't bad times. There were. Sometimes, it seemed like that was all there was. But, dammit, when the clouds parted and the sun got caught in the fibers of your hair, and your mouth crinkled around the corners so deep the crevices threatened to swallow that little key I loved so much, well, baby, I didn't just feel good. I felt like the whole world was symphonies and pop songs pouring out of my ears. That kind of love ain't no joke, even though it cracked me up so bad sometimes, I couldn't breathe.

"It was all hormonal," Asmoff said, after days or years of this kind of talk. "It was all chemicals. I could tell you exactly what atoms were vibrating at what frequencies that caused you to feel that way. I could rearrange them even if I wanted."

"I don't have any hormones. I don't have anything. I'm not a body anymore, I'm a—what did you call it?—a temp—temporary, no that's not right—a tamb— "

"Non-Temporal Echo of Consciousness," Asmoff said.

"I think we'd call it a soul on Earth," I said.

"Sounds like you had goofy ideas about all sorts of things down there," Asmoff said.

"Whatever—like I was saying—I don't have those vibrating atoms anymore. I've got nothing. Except for love."

"Echoes of chemical reactions. Mere memories of a breeding impulse. Vestigial organs from a previous existence," Asmoff said.

"*Love*," I said. "It's the only thing I can think about. We were supposed to be together. Supposed to live a long life, as partners, just loving each other. It was supposed to be us. I was supposed to kiss that key mouth every morning, and every night, for decades. And if there's an afterlife, I'm damn-well supposed to be spending it with him, and not out here with whatever you are."

"Supposed to, supposed to, supposed to," Asmoff said. When it shook its head asteroids and stardust drifted down from the galaxies on its antlers like dandruff. "Nothing is supposed to happen. The universe doesn't owe you anything. The universe doesn't even know you exist, much less care."

"And how would you know?" I snapped.

"Because before you showed up here, I didn't know you existed. And I certainly didn't care."

"If that's the case, then screw the universe. And screw you, too." I said, then lapsed into silence. A silence that could have been fifteen minutes, or could have been a day. Only Asmoff seemed to understand how time worked at the center of things. For me, it was a mess. No matter where I was, with you gone, it was a mess.

"Maybe the universe didn't owe us anything. Maybe it didn't have a plan for us. But we did. We owed ourselves. We had plans. We were each other's' others. And we knew and we cared. And that was enough to make it matter. To make it true," I said.

"Christ. You really think so, don't you?"

I stared it down as a comet shot across its one eye, disappeared under the bridge of its nose, and resurfaced in the next eye.

"If, say, you were to go back—back to the very beginning of life, with a new body, a new mind, a new everything, you think it would happen all over again? That you two would fall in love, and you could make it work?"

"I know it would. We would. For sure," I said. "I'd bet on it a thousand times. Ten thousand times, even."

"So, it's a wager then," Asmoff said.

The second time, I seek you out before we're even out of elementary school. You weren't the you I loved before, and I was not that first me. We'd been rewritten at a molecular level. And yet, you still had that little key, this time perched on your left pinky finger.

Even without it, I would have known you, though. I felt a pull the moment I came out of the womb. A singular drive to find you, love you, and never let harm come to us again. It was there from the start; a hot, iron cord wrapped around my ribcage, pulling me in your direction. It was love.

The first time I saw you was on the playground during recess. Your hair was pulled up into lopsided pigtails, and you were sucking on your fingers. You pulled them out with a wet schlucking sound and looked at me as I approached.

"You wanna play house? you asked. I nodded wordlessly. You

took my dry hand in your wet one, and lead me to the jungle gym, and the world became nothing more or less than Doo-Wah-Diddie, set to the tempo of my heart.

In high school I gave you a jacket and a promise ring. We went to the movies, to prom, and nuzzled behind the Steak and Shake on Saturday nights. We were talking futures and colleges and everything was just Do-Wah-Diddy Diddy-Dum Diddy-Doo so loud that I didn't notice when you'd stopped singing along. I didn't notice you packing one bag, buying one ticket. I didn't notice as you left, crying softly and quietly, into the small, insignificant vastness of Earth's inky night. I didn't notice a thing until all I had to listen to was my own voice, reading your goodbye note.

I'd loved you too early. I loved you too hard. Or maybe I forgot love wasn't a line we had to follow from point A to point B. It was a diving board that could launch us into an ocean of possibilities.

You were scared, you said. You only had one life.

And in a sense, that was true for you, I suppose. This you would only be this you this one time.

And in a sense it was true for me, too. Because all my lives were tied into one continuous strand by my love for you.

When you're longing for someone, seconds span the rise and fall of empires, and decades are just sighs. I picked up smoking and became a substitute teacher. I loved schools, now that they were a place where I'd spent most of my time with you. I checked in on you through shared acquaintances a few times. You got married. Never had kids.

When I was forty-six, and up to two packs a day, you ran into me outside of a gas station when you were visiting home. You covered your face with your hands and stared at me through the space between your wedding ring and the key birthmark.

"It's you," you said, shaking. "It's you."

We came together like two storm fronts.

Later you stuck your fingers in my mouth and I sucked the wedding ring clear off and spat it to the floor. You framed my face with your hands and brought it to your mouth like it was a pitcher of water and you'd lived the last twenty years in the desert, and baby, oh, baby it was Doo-Wah-Diddy Diddy-Dum, Diddy-Doo.

And sometimes it was fights over bills, or socks on the floor, or who said or did what jerkass thing. There was a year and a half devoted to your hellish divorce. And there were two years where I'd cry every time I saw a taxi that looked a certain way, and you were so mad because it meant we either had to move, or spend a small fortune on tissues.

But every time our music got too low, and the outside noise too much, I'd reach across and take your hand. I'd rub the key on your finger. I'd remember the long, empty stretch of years before I found you again. The smoking, the drinking, and the staring blankly at nothing until my eyes closed themselves. I'd remember first-you, laying bloody across my lap while the paramedics' sirens blared and blared and blared, ten minutes, too late, too late, too much, too bad. Too, too bad.

I'd check your eyes for Asmoff then, and I'd hold my head to your chest until your heartbeat became a drum track, and the world started to sing again.

Then one day while I was putting away groceries and you were running a bath, something happened inside my skull. A kind of fluttering, like a moth was trying to beat its way out of my head. Then I couldn't hear anything. No Do-Wahs or sirens. I couldn't see anything, either. The world was a colorless, soundless nothing.

But I could feel your lips against the back of my hand, moving, softly. Over and over. I could feel the words.

The time—the wasted time.

And I love you, I love you, I love you. Come back.

Until your lips got tired, and then all I could feel were tears.

Who was I after that? Was I the first me, or the second? I couldn't tell you then. I can't even give you an exact answer now. All I know is that between lives, I'm me. Every single me I've ever been, and all the potential me`s I ever could be, and also none of them, all at once.

What I can tell you is I came back shaking and crying the way souls do; with every single shadow of an atom I had.

"You're back," Asmoff said. "I'm a little surprised. I wasn't sure you'd end up back here to be honest."

I sobbed, and I ached, and knew out there, light years away and eons ago, you were doing the same, and that made me sob and ache all the more. Asmoff sighed and waited for it to subside. When it finally did, I looked at Asmoff with tears still in my eyes.

"I guess I'm stuck with you," Asmoff said. "Tell me, how was it?"

"Send me back," I said.

"Tell me how it was first," Asmoff said. "We need to judge who won, keep a tally, and all that. This is, after all, a wager."

"It's torture," I said.

"I thought you said it was love," Asmoff replied.

"Fuck you."

"Oh please. You don't know what torture is until you've spent all of eternity alone at the center of nothing, watching everything drift away from you. Now, tell me, how was it?"

"It was wonderful," I began, and by the time I finished, Asmoff was sitting in sullen silence, its eyes as black, thick, and dull as primordial tar.

"Let's see how well it works out if you don't remember this time," Asmoff said. "Let's leave it to chance completely, shall we? See how your love works out then."

Here's what love is; it's the warmth, and relaxation, and abandon that tricks you into spending an extra fifteen minutes laying in the sun, even though you know you're already burning.

That first point went to me. The second one, too. My soul seeks you out, without my body knowing why. We spend a mundanely wonderful life together as a banker and a bookseller in Italy, before lung cancer takes you away from me.

I don't actively try to die, but I don't last long after you go. I never do.

The third. The fourth. Mine.

Each time I come back, I feel like my skin has been chipped off inch by inch. I feel like someone has reached into my throat and pulled my stomach inside out. I feel like I'm back on that street, and you've just been hit, and I'm holding you. My hands are going all over. And I know. I know I could save you, God dammit, if I could just stop the blood. I could save us, if I could just get my hands on life and wrestle it back into your body.

And then there's Asmoff. In your eyes. In the emptiness of space. Alone, and waiting for me.

Asmoff takes the fifth. I don't take the right amount of time in between. I come back feeling too raw. This time it's harder to hear the music when we touch. It's hard to hear anything other than the screech of tires and blaring paramedic sirens.

"This is over," I tell you, during a fight that should have remained mostly innocuous. "Get the fuck out."

For a few days I feel free. Like the whole universe has opened up in front of me.

And then, the rain falls a certain way and splatters against my hand and I hear *Doo-Wah-Diddie, the waste, oh the waste*, and my heart is sick for the rest of my life.

I look everywhere and never find you. I develop a fever while living out of a Motel 6. In the bathroom mirror, I catch sight of Asmoff in my pupils, beckoning me. Waiting. Laughing.

Come home, it says.

After that one, I float in space for a thousand years, while Asmoff tells me how every other life had been a fluke.

"It was never anything special," Asmoff said.

While my heart was sick, I believed it. I wasted time, sulking. I pretended to forget.

But inevitably, that iron cord was still there, woven into the particles of what makes up my being, stretching across the universe to wrap around the neck of your little key.

No matter how it hurt, I just couldn't stay away.

"Tell me more about how it works—electricity," Asmoff said,

rolling me over in space to face it. It saw that I was crying for the first time in a hundred years, and frowned.

"Not this again." Asmoff said

"Send me back," I said.

Here's what love is: a roller coaster that hasn't passed inspection yet.

346-23; We're migrant workers, we're poor, and I spend six years drinking too much, during which you spend two with someone else, but none of that matters in the end. I get clean, you come back, and fuck, baby, it's beautiful the way we fit our tired, used bodies into the bed together at night.

"It's cruel to run off right when you get back, you know. While you're down there with them, I'm up here all alone, you know. You could take some time to talk to me at least, you know."

"Send me back."

516-29: Before I can get to you, an addiction does. The first time I see your face is next to your obituary. Asmoff has sent me back without full consciousness this time. Even still, I cry for weeks without ever knowing why, and never marry.

Asmoff reached into its eye and pulled out a stone the size of its finger nail.

"I could build you a whole planet, right here. I could build it however you like. You say it, and I'll do it. I can even make animals. I can make other people. I can make you your own Earth."

Asmoff crushed the stone into a cluster of small rocks and set them circling around a nearby star. "You can even pick which one you want to live on. I'll be right here, watching. I can give you ten thousand guaranteed-good lives. I can give you even *more*."

"Will they be there?" I asked.

Asmoff stared at me, and I stared back.

It waved its hand, sending the planets spinning off into the nothingness of space like tops.

"You're going to regret this," it said. A star rolled to the brim of its murky eye and pressed against the surface. White mist rippled around the impact site, before the star broke free and rolled down Asmoff's cheek.

"Send me back," I said.

968-30: We spend a perfect life together as frogs living in a shallow canal that runs along the highway. I catch you a bouquet of flies for our first date. You let me tongue the green key-shaped spot on your back. We dig holes in the cool mud, side by side, and we croak together. Our voices meld into a seamless, everlasting song. We compose it every second of every night, with every blink of our big, dopey, moon-filled eyes, every brush off our slick, goopy skin, and every bulge of our blooming throats.

It's our song, and it's perfect.

One night, while we're singing our way back to each other across the expanse of road, a taxi rolls over your precious, small body, and my voice is left alone. A week later, I let the hot summer sun cook the life out of me.

"It hurts you," Asmoff screams. "It hurts you. It hurts you. Why don't you care that it hurts you? Why won't you stop?"

"They're my person."

"Anyone can be your person. Anyone. I could make you a million persons. I could keep you safe from this—this—*love*," Asmoff reaches out, but it's too big to hold me. Even when it closes its fist, I'm still drifting in a world's worth of empty space inside its palm.

"Please," Asmoff says, peering at me through the circle of its fingers. "I don't understand."

"Yes, you do. You do," I say. "Send me back."

Stars are pouring out of Asmoff. They're cresting the film over its eyes one by one, shooting milky ripples across their surfaces until they`re churning with the force of a tsunami. The stars drip into its palm until I am floating alongside an entire constellation. The last star drops into place as I'm pulled back through space. The constellation takes shape.

A key.

"Come back," Asmoff says. "Please. Come back."

Here's what love is; It's you and me, and we're building a house together. The blueprints are no good. Water spilled on them and smudged the upper right quarter. W*here the bedroom is supposed to be*, I say, and I reach out to pinch your butt. You throw the blueprints to the side and admit that you never knew how to read them, anyway. Still, we build. At first it's so small, we can't help but get in each other's way, and smell the stink of each other's feet. But we keep building. Sometimes I slack off and slip out the back to sneak a cigarette and drink coffee, and sometimes you worry that it's all wrong, and it'd be better to just burn it all down and go start over on another plot of land. We both snap at one another, and hammers miss nails, and sometimes hit thumbs. But we build. It gets bigger every day. Inside there are libraries big enough to fit every love story known to mankind, plus all the ones that only we know about. There are as many mattresses, quilts, couches, and pillows as there have been soft words between us. There are photographs, dirty socks and breakfast dishes, and the non-temporal echoes of planet sized kisses. We stop building but find there's still work to be done. There is always work to be done. Some rooms are drafty, some have holes in the wall, or are built at a slant. Sometimes, the plumbing malfunctions, the place floods, and all the bad shit rises to the top. Sometimes, it seems too big, too messy, too much, and maybe we start wanting something newer, cleaner and simpler. Or sometimes, despite its size, we feel pent up, like we're suffocating, and we just want to go outside and getaway to anywhere else. But at the end of the day, it's a place you and I built together, baby, and it's home. It's our center. No matter where else I go, I'm gonna wanna come back.

I'm always gonna wanna come back.

THE CENTER OF EVERYTHING

I'LL TELL YOU A LOVE STORY

Acknowledgments

First, I would like to thank my mother, Janet Ann Chapin-Johnson, and my father, Amos Walter "Jay" Johnson, for being the kind of parents willing to encourage their child's art and imagination. My mother, as a hippie, taught me to believe in dragons, fairies, the impossible, and above all, myself. My father, as a musician, taught me the passion that goes into making art of any kind. Both, as avid readers, taught me how to love a good story.

Next, I'd like to thank Christopher Barzak, who is the best teacher, mentor and friend that a budding author could hope for. It's no stretch to say that without his encouragement and guidance, this book never would have existed, and I never would have become the author I am today—or likely any sort of author at all. He never failed to provide the validation and motivation I needed to keep going when I was ready to throw in the towel. He's been an invaluable source of help and wisdom when it comes to not only to writing, but to life itself, and in many ways, I'd have been lost without him. To Mr B., I'd like to express my deep gratitude and love. You're a special kind of teacher, author, and person.

I'd like to thank Bridgette Lewis, who stuck with me and managed a 13 hour time difference so that we could keep on workshopping, talking, and supporting each other while we were on opposite sides of the globe. She's one of the strongest, most determined, and best authors I know, and I admire and love her greatly. I'm honored that she was the first to see most of these stories, and the first to see the book all together as a whole.

I'd like to thank Brigitta Albares and Matthew Lattanzi, both of whom helped me discover my voice during graduate school, and with whom I had some of my best times. Matthew Lattanzi, while he may be gone, will never be forgotten, and his gentle heart and his narrative flair has left a permanent impact on me in more ways than I can express. I'd also like to give thanks to Caleb Sarvis and the rest of the Bridge Eight team for their hard work and help putting this collection out. I'd like to extend my gratitude to everyone who supported and impacted me during my adolescence as an author and person; Donna Wesner, Joelle Pecnik Barath, Dan Barath, and the rest of the coven; thanks for tolerating me during my teens and early twenties, Dave Drogowski, Mike Gismondi, Ben Reese, Brigid Cassin and the Rust Belt Writers, Karen Schubert, Tom Pugh, Chris Lettera, Chris Brady, Bill Soldan, Alex Puncekar, Travis Craig, Dr. Tiffany Anderson, Dr. William Greenway, Mindi Greenway, Cynthia Vigliotti, Imad Rahman, Catherine Wing, Guy Shebat, Dr. Linda Strom, Stephen Smith, Kate Graff, Cherise Benton, Josh Briones, and Sarah Bauman. I'd like to thank Marquesse Shine, who one of the kindest and most creative people I ever knew, Jacob Webb, for being someone I could gently rough and tumble with as a youth, and Alia Hajaj who was always bright, colorful, and unique. Case, for helping me stay sane with our long distant talks. And, of course, William D'Avignon, who is the best kind of friend a person could ask for, and someone I'll always love dearly.

    I'd also like to thank those that helped me adjust to living abroad in Japan. Laura Plaisted and Geoff Harris, thanks for taking time out to read my fiction and to support me in a strange land. Chris Tersorio, who I had the best times with, and who was always there in his wild way. I'd like to thank Matsuura Masamichi, who took me in as family and shared not only his culture with me, but so many laughs. He's one of the kindest and most interesting people I know, and I'm lucky he's my Japanese dad. I'd also like to thank the rest of my Kagawa family; Megumi Sawarame, Akiko Ishikawa, Yui Ishihama, and James Barbosa. A special thanks to Haru, aka Tony, aka DJ No Money, for being my best friend despite being ten years old, as well as the rest of the Gem students. To those who fought the good fight, Deborah Winfield, Arian Cato, Jason Alonzo, Dominique Rowinkski, Jared Welch, Alyssa DeSimone, and all the rest, those were some wild times and it was an honor to work beside you. Rise up.

    I'd also like to thank everyone who made me feel welcome in Okayama; Lona Ulsame, Amaleah Romero Cepe, Shuana Clarke, Joahnamay Kato, Diane Hasegawa, Mr. Sugihara, Johnny Govea, and Scott Dippie. Thanks to all the teachers at Chayamchi Elementary School who were so kind and friendly despite my baby Japanese; Mr. Shohei Nishimura and Mr. Yuichi Haga, who were above and beyond helpful, Ms. Kyoko Katayama, Ms. Yoko Kitabatake, Ms. Naoka Miyasako, Mr. Kazuaki Takahashi, Ms. Yuko Furuichi, Mr. Kazuya Mitani, Ms. Asaka Ishida, Ms. Kaho Sawai, Mr. Yukihiro Gouda, Ms. Kayako Inoue, Ms. Yuko Kobayakawa, Principal Tadashi Tyuta, and Ms. Naomi Ito, who had a great sense of style and humor. And, of course, I'd also like to thank my students for all their high-fives and hard work, and for being a driving factor in why Japan was such a special place for me. And last, but certainly by far not least, I'd like to give my thanks to Jude O'Brien, who became one of my best friends, and helped me find my feet while I learned to live again. I owe you so much more than just a futon.

In her poem, "The Uses of Sorrow," Mary Oliver wrote: "Someone I loved once gave me a box full of darkness. It took me years to understand this too, was a gift." Working on this collection helped me unpack my own boxes, and here at the end, I'm ready to express my gratitude for those gifts as well.

Thanks everyone for everything. I really mean it.